A BURNING QUESTION . . .

Who was the killer? Lyon kept asking himself that question as his balloon drifted high above the Connecticut River. Suddenly he had it! The whole thing fit! Now with this last piece of information, the killer's identity could be *proved*. He looked around for a place to land.

Suddenly a two-engine Cessna headed straight for him. As the plane passed over the balloon, liquid poured down. A drop fell on Lyon's hand. He tasted it—gasoline! Fear stabbed him. He could see a hand extended from the pilot's window with a flare gun poised. His scream was drowned by a deafening roar as the top of his balloon burst into raging flames. . . .

SCENE OF THE CRIME ® MYSTERIES

MURDER INK ® MYSTERIES

A Scene Of The Crime® Mystery

A CHILD'S GARDEN OF DEATH

Richard Forrest

A DELL BOOK

Published by
Dell Publishing Co., Inc.
1 Dag Hammarskjold Plaza
New York, New York 10017

Dell ® TM 681510, Dell Publishing Co., Inc.

ISBN: 0-440-11325-3

Reprinted by arrangement with the author
Printed in the United States of America

First Dell printing—May 1982

FOR
MARY BOLAN BRUMBY

One

"Who the hell is Sonja Henie?"

The young police officer turned from the grave. His outstretched hand held tongs which grasped the neck of the mottled and decomposed doll. In macabre unison the others in semi-circle around the pit followed his slow movements.

"Bag and label it before you drop the Goddamn thing," Chief Rocco Herbert said.

With his free hand the young officer snapped open a plastic film bag and abruptly dropped the doll inside. As the doll slid down the smooth surface a small skate crumpled into fine dust.

"You're breaking the Goddamn evidence," Rocco Herbert snapped.

"Sorry, sir," the young officer replied as he gently rolled the top of the bag shut and sealed the opening. "But Sonja Henie?"

"Yes, I would think so," Lyon Wentworth said, while still staring into the excavation at their feet. He looked up at the circle of expectant faces. "The doll seems to have on ice skates and is made of a type of molded composition used during World War II when rubber was scarce and before plastics. In the forties Sonja Henie dolls were very popular with children."

"That might help," Chief Herbert said. "If that is a family in there."

They looked back into the shallow pit. The dirt surrounding the three skeletons had been carefully re-

RICHARD FORREST

moved and the final particles brushed away with extreme care. They were huddled together with jaws gaping in silent conversation. Moments before, the smallest's arms had been clutching the remnants of the doll; but now the bones were pushed askew in a beseeching gesture.

"The little one . . . it's a girl, isn't it?" Lyon asked.

"I don't know," Rocco replied.

Lyon Wentworth was sorry he had come. Chief Rocco Herbert's phone call of two hours ago had at first annoyed him. He hated disruptions while working. Once the train of thought was broken, his curiosity had been piqued.

"It's probably an old settlers' burial area," he had said.

"When they first called me I yelled cow bones," Rocco replied. "But now that I've seen them, they're not that old. Christ, Lyon! Three of them. We haven't had anything like that in Murphysville since the last Indian raids."

A cool spring breeze came over the ridge top and blew a fine film of dirt across the grave. Lyon felt a chill and didn't know if it was caused by the breeze penetrating the light jacket he'd thrown on as he left the house, or by the things before him.

He was a tall, angular man of forty. The wind rustled a forelock of blond-browning hair, and he pushed it back with his palm in an often repeated gesture. Lyon Wentworth wore tennis sneakers without socks, denim work pants, the light jacket covering a green sport shirt. His face seemed to have a slightly troubled look, but one that could instantaneously change to a wide and warm smile.

He turned again to the silent police chief next to him. "Any idea of how long they've been in there?"

"Not yet. The medical people might come up with something, but I wanted you to see it before we moved anything."

"Missing persons?"

"Nothing yet, but we haven't much to go on. If you're right about the doll, they've been in there thirty years."

Lyon turned back to the grave as a photographer scuttled halfway into the pit to get some angled shots. The three skeletons nestling in the bottom of the hole gaped up at them with boned grimaces as if resenting the intrusion on their rest. "One's missing an arm," Lyon said.

"Over there, beyond the bulldozer," Chief Herbert said. "It must have been outstretched or raised in some manner. The 'dozer blade caught and carried it a few feet before the operator realized what he had. That's when he called me."

"Your men cleared the rest of the dirt away?"

"Yes."

"Anything else? Weapon, shovel, anything?"

"No. We've combed the area for two hundred yards in every direction, but if it's been thirty years, I wouldn't expect to find anything. Nothing, just the grave, three bodies, the doll, a few shreds of cloth left from their clothing; nothing else. Except, they were probably clobbered with something heavy: each skull is filled with fractures. It doesn't take any expert pathologist to see that."

"And that's all?" Lyon asked again tiredly.

"Afraid so, Lyon," Rocco said. "Not much to go on

unless the medical and lab people turn up something, or by some miracle an old missing persons report is able to fill us in."

Lyon looked into the grave for the last time and turned away. "I've seen enough."

The Chief turned to the waiting officers. "All right, move it, but for God's sake be careful."

They started to do his bidding and then poised in silent tableau as the sound of sirens wavered and died. Four State Police cruisers stopped on the road below them. Car doors slammed in unison as troopers started up the hill, led by a red-faced captain.

"Christ!" Rocco said. "Here comes the cavalry."

Lyon noticed that activity around the grave site had ceased as the young police officers watched the approaching entourage in a guilty manner, like small boys caught in some mischievous act. Ten yards away the trooper captain, puffing slightly from the exertion of the climb up the hill, began to yell at Rocco Herbert.

"Damn it all, Chief! You should have called as soon as it was discovered." The captain, now at the site, continued yelling at the tall police chief. "What do you have up here? The whole Murphysville force?"

"Just the day shift," Rocco replied.

The trooper captain glared into the grave. "Probably Indian graves. The boys at the lab will run it down."

"You're in the confines of Murphysville, Norbert," Rocco said.

The red-faced captain ignored the remark and gestured toward Lyon. "Who's the civilian?"

"A friend of mine," Rocco said. "Lyon Wentworth, meet my brother-in-law, Captain Norbert."

The captain seemed to shake hands with Lyon automatically while still glaring into the grave. "You've probably mucked up any evidence there was."

"Damn it, Norbert, we haven't mucked up anything. I've been to the FBI school the same as you have," the police chief replied angrily.

"Of course you're calling the state in—officially."

Rocco paused slightly before answering. "No, not yet. I'll need you for the lab and pathology work, but that's all for now."

"Listen, Rocco, you aren't prepared to handle this and you know it."

"For the time being it's a Murphysville matter," Rocco said and walked away, only to be followed by the captain. Away from the group the heated but subdued argument continued while state troopers glared across the grave at the uniformed police.

Lyon Wentworth walked down the incline of the rough-cut road the bulldozer had been slicing before its ghoulish discovery. He could hear the heavy tread of Rocco Herbert behind him and he quickened his pace. A spring zephyr touched his face as he looked through the trees at the clear sky, and he wondered if he'd have a chance to get a flight in this Sunday.

The Chief caught up to him at the stone wall that ran along the country lane, and he placed a large hand on Lyon's shoulder. Lyon turned to look into the taller man's eyes.

"I need your help, Lyon," the Chief said.

The bond between them had lasted for a number of

years, and the large hand on Lyon's shoulder seemed inchoately to transmit this. Although Lyon was tall, Rocco Herbert was taller by several inches. He was a large man of huge dimensions, six feet eight inches, with a solid girth of 270 pounds. His face was deeply chiseled, capable of a foreboding visage and yet also warmth and humor.

"You're personalizing this thing, Rocco. Let the State Police handle it."

"This is the biggest thing we've had here in years—it's a chance for me to move out of the force."

Lyon smiled. "The ways of justice move in an odd manner."

"You want I should kid you?"

"I want you should leave me alone. Come on, Rocco, what kind of help could I possibly be?"

"I'm not sure. I only know that you think in strange ways, and this is going to be strange . . . like that business with the doll."

"So, now you're offering me a puzzle?"

"Like in the old days," the big man replied.

Lyon sighed. "There's so little to go on."

"I know, except for the doll, and that could have belonged to anyone. An itinerant farm family up here to work the tobacco fields. . . ."

"I don't think so," Lyon said. "Those Madam Alexander dolls are an expensive make and cost from eight to ten dollars even thirty years ago. Hardly what an itinerant worker could afford in those days."

"We could try a trace on the doll . . ."

"I don't think so. You know, the family could have been from out-of-state, passing through . . . killed by a hitch-hiker."

14

"I know," the Chief said. He sat on the wall, his back to the road, looking up the gradually sloped hill where police formed a hive of activity at the grave site. His voice was sad. "All the informers, computers and legword in the world won't help on this one. How, Lyon? How in the hell do you find a murderer if you don't know who the victims are?"

"I don't know, Rocco." He sat on the stone wall next to the large police officer, and they both let their gaze wander from the grave toward the clear Connecticut afternoon sky. "I really don't know, but that's your job."

"It's a miracle they were found, even today. This area is rural, the real boonies. Thirty years ago it must have been the ends of the earth."

"Why the bulldozer out here?"

"A developer."

"Here, in the middle of nowhere?"

"I thought maybe you knew about it. A group is planning to build a large condominium retirement village out here. Natural setting, homes built in the hillside, clusters, retain all the natural beauty, all that sort of thing. Thank God the 'dozer operator didn't have a hangover and saw what in hell he was slicing through."

"You might have been better off if they'd left it the way it was."

"That's a hell of a thing to say."

"Don't involve me, Rocco."

"I need this one, Lyon. My finale, my swan song. If this thing is handled properly, I can retire, and now that Garfland's gone, I can run for town clerk."

RICHARD FORREST

"You've got your own force and a couple thousand state police you can call on."

'The Murphysville Police Force boasts twelve men, and that includes writing traffic tickets, school grade crossings, and trying to keep Hinkle sober."

"I've always been interested in your work, Rocco. But I'm not a professional. And besides—I'm working on a project."

"That child in the grave up there would be about the same age as . . ."

"Come on, Rocco."

The large man beside Lyon looked instantly remorseful. Although his daughter, Remley, was Lyon's goddaughter, unspoken between them was a spring day years ago.

An instant picture transformed the country lane before him.

A little girl, skirt billowing in the wind as she pedals furiously on her new bike as he turns and goes back into the house on the Green. Lyon stood . . . and the picture was gone.

The Chief's voice softened. "She liked your last book."

"Which one?"

"The Monster on the Mantel. What's the new one?"

"The Cat in the Capitol. And I intend to finish it."

"Finish it in your spare time."

"That's my livelihood you so blithely give away."

They were standing face to face, and a slight twist of the police officer's lips betokened the good humor Lyon knew lurked just below the surface.

"You've just never realized that it isn't Korea anymore, Chief."

16

"For God's sake, that was more years ago than I care to remember."

"Agreed." In the slightly graying but huge police chief before him, Lyon could still see the young ranger captain of twenty years before. They had met accidentally in division headquarters. Lyon was the youngest Assistant G-2 in FECOM and Rocco Herbert a recently promoted ranger captain and company commander. In those days, from that time, Rocco and his ranger company became Lyon's eyes and ears. They foraged behind enemy lines, acted as point company, and constantly fed information back in an orderly and complete manner. They made an excellent team, and higher command seemed to sense this strange alliance between the all-American tackle and gruff ranger officer and the almost effete Lyon, who, although commissioned as an Infantry officer, never served with a line company.

They had operated as an effective team, as if a strange symbiotic relationship transcended each of them and allowed the sums of their parts to become a force larger than each individually.

Rocco Herbert kicked at the stone wall. "I swear to Christ," he said, "I'm going back to resign. Even watching rock festivals is better'n this."

"Retire, run a security force at some plant and get fat."

"Screw you," the Chief said and kicked the wall again.

"Every time you kick that wall you knock a rock off. Do you know the work it took to build that thing one hundred and fifty years ago?"

They both looked down the shaded road and the

wall that stretched its length for several hundred yards. "Poor bastards," Rocco said reflectively.

"Who? The ones who built the wall?"

"No. The ones on the hill up there."

They contemplated the hill in the quiet day. Occasional distant murmurs from men working at the grave site could be heard. The road behind them ran through the bed of the valley, a small stream on the other side of the road, and the hill before them rose in a gentle slope from the wall to traprock crest. Once, years ago, cleared and utilized as dairy pasture. Now, covered with second-growth timber and spotted with glacier boulders too large to be moved to the wall site.

The grave far up the hill several hundred yards from the road was near the ridge top, and that bothered Lyon. He began to think about that while Rocco waited patiently.

"Something's wrong," Lyon said. "It doesn't fit."

"What's that?" Rocco replied, trying to hide the eager lilt to his voice.

"I don't think they were killed here, but were transported and buried."

Rocco thought a moment. "Possibly."

"The configuration of the hill." Lyon lapsed into silence again. "Whose land is this? Who would use it, walk over it?"

"It's part of Water Company property. Just recently they sold off this side of the ridge to the condominium developer. I doubt that anyone's been here in years except for hunters."

"Hunters. Yes," Lyon said. "In the past fifty years they're probably the only ones who have walked this land."

"Not picturesque enough for tourists, no trail for hikers, too wild for lovers."

Lyon continued looking up the hill. Except for the naked cut made by the bulldozer that had unearthed the bodies, the hillside was close to virginal. "Pheasant country," he said.

"An occasional deer," the Chief replied.

The location of the grave, the wild aspect of the hill—something in that combination bothered Lyon. He turned toward Chief Herbert. "Too far up the hill."

"What?"

"Why would he bury them that far up the ridge when a few yards in from the road would have been adequate?"

"He? Yeah—probably was a man. Offhand I can't recall any women mass murderers bashing in the collective skulls of whole families. At least not since Lizzie Borden. But as far as the distance up the hill, he was probably just cautious."

"That's a long way to lug three bodies for caution's sake."

"Not if he didn't want them found for thirty years—or ever."

"Perhaps," Lyon mused. "Perhaps."

"That's not much to go on," Rocco said. "A five-state missing persons search, maybe something from the physical evidence. Not much, Lyon."

The descending sun reflected orange globes on the windshields of the line of police cruisers. A man's deep laugh echoed across the valley from the grave site and Lyon wondered what could be humorous in that small plot, that garden of death. His car waited and he wanted to leave, to be away from this place with its shattered secret which cast a foreboding aura over the valley.

He turned toward the expectant chief. "We're having a few people over to the house Monday night. Why don't you and Martha stop in?"

"We'd like to," the police officer replied. "Are you sure there's no chance we can do something with that doll?"

"I know you'll try, Rocco, but I doubt it."

"Jesus, I don't know where in hell to start."

"Another one like the girl in the fire."

"I'm afraid so, unless something unexpected turns up," Rocco said.

They both knew that Lyon referred to the body of the little girl discovered in the smoldering ruins of the Hartford circus fire. In 1944 the Ringling Brothers, Barnum and Bailey Circus tent had unexpectedly caught fire in Hartford. Within four minutes the fire had raged out of control and quickly killed over a hundred people. One of the victims was a small girl who was never identified or claimed. For several years the body was kept in a local mortuary, then finally buried. Twenty-five years later the child was still unknown and unclaimed. Rocco had once learned that newly commissioned troopers were assigned to the investigation as a sort of initiation ritual. After thousands of hours of investigation there was still no clue to the identity of the girl.

"Monday about eight," Lyon said and put an arm on the morose chief's shoulder.

"Damn it all, Lyon. Just think about it."

"I know you'll do all that can be done."

"Which won't be much."

Lyon walked toward the small red Datsun parked beyond the police cruisers, his pace becoming quite brisk as from the corner of his eye he saw a group of officers coming down the hill carrying large rubber bags.

He was compelled to turn. Two officers carried each bag, except for the smallest bag, held by the youngest officer—carried away from his body as if he were afraid of defilement.

In the car he turned the ignition too violently. The starter engine buzzed and the car stalled. Sitting back in the seat he breathed deeply and then slowly started the engine again. Turning the wheels abruptly he pulled away from the line of cruisers and accelerated quickly down the country road. The late afternoon sun spreckled through overhanging trees and cast rapidly changing patterns across his face, and he jammed the gear into fourth and felt the car jerk forward with gained momentum.

He thought again of his relationship with the large police officer. Initially a natural bond of interest between intelligence officer and ranger captain; a needed thing in a combat zone. Later, the discovery that they were both Nutmeggers, and finally R and R leave in Japan and Lyon's introduction, by the captain, into strange and erotic rites with dimpled young Japanese women.

Chief Rocco Herbert, at one time the youngest chief in the state. Still certainly the largest in physical size. The man's sheer mass aided his innate gentleness and usually precluded the necessity for him to utilize violent methods. A man who during his Army career wanted to be division food officer, and by order of senior command stayed on as ranger captain, delegated to carry out the most dangerous and necessary missions of the division.

Rocco Herbert, professional police officer whose greatest desire was election to town clerk—keeper of documents, neat and dusty volumes of deeds and mortgages—an incongruous man in a vault of records. And yet Lyon remembered his last visit to the Chief's house, a vivid picture of a man holding a small kitten in his hamlike hands, with a Colt Trooper MKV magnum revolver clipped to his belt.

They had been discharged from service almost simultaneously and their friendship had continued. Rocco, already married and a father, as the returning war hero had been unanimously offered the position of town police chief, a Bronze Star for bravery and his large size seeming to be his greatest assets.

Lyon had gone to Yale for graduate work, and even then the friendship had continued. It had been Rocco who had read the first draft of Lyon's thesis on violence in Victorian children's literature, and it was Rocco who had pointed out in clear fashion new insights that allowed Lyon to finish his work with a firm and unique slant.

The relationship continued over the years as Lyon taught English and Rocco, in an initial burst of ambition, studied law and criminology. The police chief, with his natural affinity for children and animals, was often the first reader of Lyon's books, while Lyon would listen to Rocco's enthusiastic reports of his ongoing education, an enthusiasm that began to wane over the years with the killing drudgery of mundane duties and boredom. Over the years the relationship had changed both of them; perhaps in light of what had happened to their lives, had saved each of them.

No, Lyon thought, friendship stopped at the brink of immersion into violence and death. No way. He wrenched the car violently into the fast lane of the Interstate and accelerated the sports car to eighty.

The honking car pulled alongside and broke Lyon's reverie. The state trooper, his cruiser parallel to Lyon's car, waved, and Lyon waved back. With whining siren the trooper pulled ahead of the Datsun to make quick movements in and out in front of the small car.

A glance at the speedometer showed Lyon that both cars were doing over eighty, and it suddenly occurred to him that the trooper's gestures were not a friendly salutation but an order to pull off the highway. The small car slowed with a drift onto the emergency lane and came to a halt on the shoulder. The police cruiser pulled up a few yards behind him. The trooper, shaking his head, left his car and approached Lyon's.

"I've been following you for a mile, sir. Didn't you see my lights?"

"No, officer. I didn't notice until you pulled alongside."

"You were doing over eighty."

"Yes, this thing really moves along, doesn't it?"

The trooper shook his head. "Yes, sir. May I see your license and registration? Please take them out of your wallet and hand them to me."

"I don't seem to have my wallet with me."

"The registration. Look in the glove compartment."

"No, I keep it in my wallet also."

"Are you the owner of this vehicle?"

"Yes. My name is Lyon Wentworth."

"Just a moment, please." The trooper went back to the cruiser, and Lyon could see him talking into the microphone of his radio. Lyon was annoyed at the delay and momentarily considered pulling off the shoulder, back onto the highway, but then again, he supposed that would annoy the trooper.

In a few minutes the officer was back at the car. "Your name is Wentworth, and you say you own this car."

"Of course."

"Any identification?"

"I told you, I must have left my wallet at home."

"Get out of the car."

"What?"

The revolver pointed directly at Lyon's nose. With his free hand the trooper opened the car door. "Get out." All friendliness and politeness were gone from his voice. "Out!"

Lyon slowly stepped from the car; the trooper stepped back, revolver still pointing. "What is this?" Lyon asked.

"Around. Brace." The trooper's free hand grasped Lyon's elbow and spun him toward the car. "Hands on the roof."

Lyon placed his palms on the roof of the car and leaned forward. He felt the trooper's brisk hands run across his body. My God! He was frisking him. He turned. "What in hell is this?"

"Back around." Lyon turned back to the roof of the car. "Connecticut marker number DC 7120 is registered to a Mr. Antony Horton of Saybrook."

"That's crazy. This is my car."

"A man of your age jumping a sports car. That's kid stuff."

On the small rear seat of the car Lyon could see several leather camera cases, light meters and several parcels that definitely weren't his. He had the wrong car. Simultaneously he and the trooper half-turned as a line of four Murphysville cruisers braked to a stop in front of the sports car. Chief Rocco Herbert unwound from the rear car and walked slowly back toward Lyon.

"Need help?" the Chief asked the trooper.

"A hot car, Chief. But he's clean. I'll book him at the Middletown Barracks."

"A forty-year-old man jumping a sports car. That's kid stuff," Rocco said.

"That's what I told him, sir. He must be a sickie."

"No doubt about it."

"Damn it all, Rocco. Tell this joker who I am."

"Brace, mister." The young trooper shoved him against the side of the car.

"Is that your car?" Rocco asked.

"Well, no. But it looks like mine."

"Grand Theft—Auto will get you two to five," Rocco said, and Lyon could see the twitch of one cheek as the Chief bit his lip. "However," he continued, "I might make a deal."

"Damn it all, Rocco, no deal, no blackmail."

The trooper clacked a handcuff around Lyon's right wrist and reached from the circle of police officers surrounding him, and then the cackle of Rocco Herbert as he leaned against the car in a paroxysm of gargantuan giggles.

Lyon's car pulled to a stop between the cruisers, and a very irate police photographer rushed over to examine his car.

"I know him," the Chief said to the trooper. "He's nuts, but harmless. Wrong car—mistake."

"He was speeding, sir."

"Write him on that. He's a menace on the highways," Rocco said.

"Very funny," Lyon said as the trooper undid the handcuff and the photographer handed him his car key. "Terribly funny."

"I thought so," Rocco said as he went back to his cruiser. "See you Monday."

Nutmeg Hill was built in 1780, some said by a Black Irishman who had made his fortune in the Triangle Trade. For 150 years after the death of its builder the house had been the home of a farming family who scrabbled a living from the marginal soil until younger heads left the land to make rifles and cannons in the Connecticut arms factories.

Lyon and Beatrice found it accidentally, the land overgrown, the house deathlike in its vacancy, only a few years from utter devastation by the elements and adventuresome young boys. With the first book royalties and an inheritance from Beatrice's father, they had bought the house and its adjoining hundred acres. The restoration had been expensive, and Lyon mentally visualized each room as completely consuming the royalties of a book. The study was labeled the

"Monster on the Mantel," and consequently housed, on the mantel, several of the large Wobbly dolls caricatured by a famous toymaker after the monster of the book.

The car spewed gravel from its rear wheels as he braked hastily in front of the house. Menace on the highways, he thought angrily to himself as he slammed the car door and stomped up the stairs. Grand Theft—Auto, that overgrown fuzz . . . he lurched even more angrily into his study and poured a triple finger of dry sack sherry.

The warming glow of sherry made him smile at himself. He poured another and contemplated the sacrilege of drinking good wine in hasty fashion, and then he laughed. He laughed at Rocco and he laughed at himself.

Sitting at the desk with his third sherry, he looked down at the partially completed manuscript of "Cat in the Capitol." The work seemed far away, the wiles and ways of feline protagonists very distant and at this bleak moment much too fey.

The desk faced the window, and through the large, multipaned glass he could see the winding Connecticut River below the house. At this point the river was wooded on both shores, heading toward Old Saybrook and Long Island Sound. Over the hill and across the river, beyond the ridge, not too distant as a bird flies . . . was the grave site.

He wouldn't think about it. After all, in a certain sense the view from the window housed many long-forgotten graves. Indians, Colonials, hardworking farmers. Countless lives had disappeared into the hard New England soil and traprock ridges of this land.

He thought that the Jewish myth of the seven just men was an excellent concept. Seven men of each generation bore the sufferings of mankind. A lovely thought allowing for a survival and compartmentalization. It was impossible to assimilate the suffering of mankind throughout the world. The mere bulk led to initial indignation which dissipated to lethargy. He had always imagined that Rocco Herbert had a capacity for indignation in sufficient quantity to allow him to view each case as a personal cause, as a vendetta against transgressors; and this constellation allowed a somewhat gentle man to operate successfully throughout most of his life in a milieu of potential violence. And how Rocco fought to hide these qualities.

Lyon Wentworth swiveled his chair and visually caressed the Wobblies on the mantel. The Wobblies, terrible of visage, were a cross between Gothic gargoyle and yeti. Their menace, by some miracle of toymaking, was gentle, as if they spoke to children with a quiet voice that said, "See, I'm not so terrible, and if I'm not, then perhaps the other monsters of life aren't." He was fascinated with his monsters, and wondered about the toymaker who created them.

The bottle of sherry across the room shimmered and he deliberated momentarily on the possibility of becoming pleasantly sloshed. The few he'd just had would make it difficult to work effectively. . . . Rocco, it's your fault, he thought. He should never have made the trip to the grave.

It was time to pull the room around him in a protective mantle, roll the rock against the cave entrance and immerse himself in the half-completed cat character. The phone rang. He had meant to shut it off.

"Hello, Wentworth here."

"WHERE THE HELL YOU BEEN, LYON? BEEN TRYING TO GET YOU HALF THE DAY."

Over the past two years his wife Beatrice had been slowly going deaf, and as sometimes happens with hearing impairments she compensated incorrectly by raising her voice. He would really have to convince her that she did have a slight problem—not fatal to her career, but disconcerting. He held the phone several inches from his ear. "Hi, Bea. Thought you'd be on your way home now."

"THAT'S WHY I'M CALLING," she bellowed, and he moved the phone a little farther away. In the background he could hear the clatter of voices in the Capitol corridors and knew she was probably calling from the Party caucus room, Connecticut probably being one of the few states in the Union whose legislators did not have private offices. "Going to be late," she continued.

"I'll wait and eat with you," he said.

"No, never mind. I'll grab something here. Have a very important meeting tonight with the welfare mothers. Watch it on TV."

"I'll turn it on."

"How's the work coming?" she asked.

"Terrible, that's why I went out and got laid this afternoon."

"That's nice," she yelled in return. "Keep it going."

She was engaged in conversation with a fellow legislator before the phone hit the cradle, and he felt a twinge of guilt for the small and slightly cruel practical joke he'd played on his wife. He considered her his tentacle to life, the outward one, the practical one with an oar dipped in midstream while he immersed himself in his study to create benign monsters. They both knew that friends and enemies often referred to them as Mutt and Jeff. They didn't care and were comfortable in their relationship.

Lyon also knew that his wife was becoming a political power in the state. She was a spokesperson (as she said) for welfare groups, feminists, and oddly enough some strange anti-tax groups. It was a juggling of ideals and political awareness that she somehow seemed to be able to keep going without fault and which had resulted in her election to two terms in the State House and one in the State Senate. They were considering her for Lieutenant-Governor in the next election—at least that's what some of the columnists said—but, knowing his wife, Lyon felt that she would probably take some strong stand on an issue before the convention and alienate herself from supporters.

It was dark, and he turned on the desk lamp with the realization that he hadn't eaten. He drank another sherry and made a chicken sandwich in the kitchen before returning to his desk to reread his notes.

With ivory glow they danced with the Wobblies, and he didn't know who they were.

Wobblies—monsters large and reminiscent of Rocco Herbert—grinned through whiskered snouts and danced in short leaps, while two porcelain figures, translucent and shining in the soft glow of the desk lamp, danced with delicate feet and grinned vacantly at him. The bonehand of the smallest stretched outward with invitation and command. He recoiled from the gesture and threw himself backwards in the chair.

30

Wobblies grinned again and joined furry hands with the jubilant chorus of dancing bones.

Lyon's hands gripped the chair arms in refusal of the beckoning invitation to join the figures.

He willed the Wobblies back to the mantel. Willed them and they reluctantly returned to their habitat. But they stood with curled feet and shook joyfully with malevolent grins as the knocking dance of the boned figures continued.

Room gone. His daughter stood before him—her first bike held firmly with that look of wonderment children have. "I can already ride a two-wheeler," she said. "I don't need training wheels."

He watched as she rode down the drive, and then turned to go into the house at the Green and distantly heard the ringing of the bell.

They were ringing the telephone in strange sequences. He awoke, his head bent forward over the desk, his neck cricked, the half-eaten sandwich in the plate before him. He picked up the phone.

"Lyon," Rocco's quiet voice said.

"Rocco, you Goddamn son-of-a-bitchin' fat pig, go to hell!" He slammed the phone back on the receiver and caught his thumb. He grimaced and sucked on the hurt fingernail as the phone rang again.

"What do you have?" Lyon asked as he sucked on his nail again.

"Hardly anything. One male, height at a probable five three, weight one hundred and four. One mature female, height five feet, weight one oh five. Both adults in the early or mid-thirties. One female child, age eight, weight sixty pounds. As we figured, they'd been in that pit thirty years. No other usable evidence

31

from the site. Negative on the doll and missing persons."

"That's all?"

"Odd dental work on the adult male. I'll try and have something more on that tomorrow."

"That could help."

"Any ideas?"

"No."

"Thanks, Lyon. 'Preciate it." The Chief hung up.

Lyon Wentworth stared down at the silent phone as his wife's car drove quickly up the graveled drive. Turning to meet her he saw that the boned dream figures had disappeared and the Wobblies sat in silent contemplation on the mantel, and he shook his head in resignation.

Two

Beatrice Wentworth glared at her husband as she entered the barn. Her look indicated less malice than a frowning puzzlement that transmitted itself to an impatient kick. She was a tallish, slight woman with close-cropped hair and darting energetic eyes. Her trim figure, now in tight slacks and fitted shirt, was slender and well proportioned.

"YOU AREN'T GOING TO RUIN ANOTHER SUNDAY BY GOING UP IN THAT THING?" she asked with arms akimbo as Lyon carried equipment from the barn.

"Only a short flight," he replied, almost dropping the propane burner.

"The last time you said that, I had to pick you up on the Boston Commons."

"I couldn't help it—the wind shifted."

"Finish your book so we can remodel the kitchen."

"I will, I will," he puffed as he dollied the bag through the barn's double doors and over to the pulley rig Rocco had helped him design and build. "Will you follow me?" he asked her.

"I had better," she replied. "If I hadn't that time you blew over the Sound, you'd probably have landed in the Azores."

"Good. How about giving me a hand?"

With Bea's help and the aid of Rocco's two-by-four network and pulley system, Lyon was able to position the balloon bag and light the propane burner. Slowly the bag began to fill with hot air, its creased folds starting to bend outward and take shape.

They stood back from the filling balloon, occasionally darting up to unfold some material so it would fill properly. Bea put her arms around him and spoke in a tone lower than he'd heard in weeks.

"You know," she said, "I wish you wouldn't go up in that thing. It scares me to death."

"I didn't know it was possible to frighten the indomitable Beatrice Wentworth."

"Things that go off the ground are frightening. I'd rather take on eight members of the opposition and two primary fights than fly from here across the river in that thing."

"Then you won't fly with me in my drifting machine?"

"Never. I'll follow in the pick-up and retrieve you from the idiotic places where you persist in landing."

The bag had filled to its outermost circumference, the large painted Wobbly head on the bag's side taking shape as the seams straightened. The Wobbly on the balloon looked more gruesome than the dolls in the study, and Lyon recalled the rather startled glances he'd often gotten from low-flying private planes.

"With luck," he told Bea, "I'll be flying due east and will come down in the Portland fairgrounds. I want to take some pictures of an area near there."

"The grave site?"

"Yes."

"Your big friend gets paid for that sort of thing."

Lyon shrugged as she kissed him on the cheek. "All right."

"Do what you will," his wife said.

The upright balloon was straining against its retaining and mooring ropes, and Lyon adjusted the propane burner and released some excess hot air through the envelope. The small, light gondola danced three feet in the air as he carefully loaded a CB radio, camera, and wide-angle lens into the compartment of the basket.

"Well, I'm off to see the Wizard," he said and stepped into the basket. "Cast off, crew."

Bea waved and scurried around the two-by-four framework, casting off lines as the balloon began gently to rise into the sky. At fifty feet the long mooring line was still held firmly by Bea on the ground, and part of the line's end, as a back-up, was attached to a powerful winch, a safety precaution he'd never had to utilize. With fine weather, like today, Lyon felt secure in the hot air balloon. The only possibility of danger was the lack of a strong mooring crew to help guide his descent in case of an immediate problem with the integrity of the envelope bag.

The lift proceeded normally and gently as the propane burner chugged and heated the air that rose through the open appendix. Lyon began to make preliminary flight checks.

As an orthodox balloonist, he still retained the wicker basket, little different from the one used in the first ascent made by Pilatre de Rozier in 1783. Looking straight upward, he noted that the nylon net surrounding the envelope was secure and taut and that the fastenings of the suspension lines to the basket ring just over his head were of proper tension. He gently grasped the valve line and, looking upward through the envelope, gave a little tug and watched to see that the valve at the apex of the envelope slid partially open. With the minute escape of air the balloon dipped slightly, and he closed the escape valve. The propane burner under the sleeve of the bottom appendix burned at the proper rate, although he increased the heat slightly to improve the ascent.

He checked the material visually around the appendix opening, making sure there were no rips or tears. He knew of one case several years ago of a fellow balloonist, intrigued with his farewells to the ground crew, who didn't notice the bottom of the appendix opening was blocked, and as the balloon rose the hot air inside expanded the bag until the balloon was torn apart with an explosion that caused an immediate crash.

He leaned over the basket and waved all clear to Bea on the ground. As she released the mooring rope he quickly reeled it into the basket. The balloon ascent increased rapidly with the mooring line drag removed.

The ripping panel was securely in place; the emergency lines, painted a bright red, were moored securely in the basket. He'd never had to use the ripping panel, usually taking care to make his ascents in clear, calm weather. In an emergency requiring rapid descent, the ripping lines could be pulled, which caused an immediate tearing away of large portions of the gas envelope, which in turn released large quantities of hot air and provided a dangerous rate of descent.

The few balloon instruments were on the right of the basket: a compass, altimeter, the variometer to record vertical movement, along with a recording barometer and a small citizens' band radio fastened tightly to the instrument panel.

At fifteen hundred feet he adjusted the burner level to maintain present altitude with little variance and for hopeful horizontal flight at that level.

"CAN YOU HEAR ME UP THERE?"

Beatrice's voice through the CB radio startled him in the silence. He threw the toggle switch on the small set. "Just fine," he said. "The winds are north-northeast. I'll meet you somewhere on the other side of the river near Portland."

"All right!"

He really would have to talk to her about having her hearing checked. Glancing over the side of the basket, he could see her below, still in the barnyard looking upward, shading her eyes. She returned his wave and started across the yard to the pick-up truck.

This was the part that made it all worthwhile. There was little to do now except maintain a check on the burner, the rate of ascent or level flight kept steady by minute adjustments between burner and escape valve. One further check on the condition of the envelope . . . and then silence except for the hiss of the burner . . . and a feeling of oneness with the sky.

Lyon's ballooning had started accidentally. In order to break his depression after the death of their daughter, Bea had pressed him to take up an outside activity. Finally, in desperation, and in order to stop her constant insistence, he had selected the most far-out activity he could imagine, taken his first lessons, and soon found himself caught up in the hobby. Now, and for the past two years, he made a flight every Sunday afternoon—weather permitting.

The balloon moved slowly over the Connecticut River. Directly below, a small coastal tanker turned toward a nearby tank farm mooring. To his right, New Haven, the Gothic tops of Yale in apposition to the newer office buildings. To the left, the city of Hartford. Below, the Connecticut River wound its way toward the Sound, visible as a large expanse immediately to his front.

He turned to see the northwest portion of the state fading into the foothills of the Berkshire mountains. Below the slowly drifting balloon now were the Connecticut Valley tobacco fields, portions of them covered by the tenting under which the tobacco could grow in high humidity.

The meteorologist at the airport had, for once, been correct. The winds at this altitude were gentle and in the optimum direction to carry him over the site.

Odd dental work on the adult male. What had they meant by that? The pathology people must have noticed something, an odd configuration in the drilling or bridgework. Something unusual they couldn't place. Dental identification would probably be impossible. Dental work done in the late thirties or early forties would probably be impossible to trace as the dentists would be either dead or retired. He knew that Rocco and the State Police would make the attempts, but any information from that source seemed highly unlikely.

Lyon switched on the five-watt CB radio. The voice transmitting on the open channel was definitely not Bea's.

"Truck Stop Two, Truck Stop Two, this is Red Ball."

"Yeah, Red Ball."

"Tell Millie I've got a layover, and we'll swing to-night."

"Gotcha', Red Ball."

My God, Lyon thought. Now, even the radio frequencies. Someday they'd discover the air, and the sky would be filled with hundreds of ballooning families, each with a transistor radio and beer cans. He tried to get Bea. "Prometheus. Can you hear me?"

"Gotcha', Prometheus," Bea answered. "What do you allow?"

He turned the sound on his set down. "Bea, would you stop at the nearest phone booth and try to get Rocco? Tell him to run a full metal assay on the fillings and bridgework of the adult male victim. There's a metal and dental supply outfit in Hartford that can do it if the state people can't."

"Gotcha', Prometheus. Stay away from rocks. Out."

His enjoyment of the flight was shattered. The intrusion of unbidden thoughts hampered any free-blown reverie. Well, to the business at hand, which was, after all, to look at the site.

The balloon drift carried it over the juncture where the country road and the Interstate highway joined. The grave site would be five miles to the east. Lyon readied camera and equipment and leaned over the basket to watch the passing ground. He reached up and released hot air through the escape valve until his height dropped and leveled at an even thousand feet. The traprock ridges were now only a few hundred feet below.

The balloon crossed the stone wall at the bottom of the hill and continued perpendicular to the rough-cut road with the bulldozer still parked where it had last stopped. A police officer guarding the site leaned against the bulldozer and looked up at the passing balloon. He waved and Lyon waved back.

On the opposite side of the hill the ridge dropped in steep incline past a logging road, down to a lake. He estimated the lake to be about 100 acres in size. He continued taking photographs as the balloon gently slid past the grave. Picture-taking complete, Lyon held onto the suspension ropes and leaned over the edge of the basket as the site disappeared from view. Something was still not right, but what?

He was eager to have the pictures developed, and now that the purpose of the flight was accomplished it was time to descend. The winds were wrong for a landing in the Portland fairgrounds, which meant he must be on the lookout for some available spot of sufficient size so as not to incur the danger of the balloon being washed against a tree line during the landing.

A half mile ahead he saw an excellent landing spot directly in his path. It had several hundred yards of open space, which was more than enough to afford a landing with the needed mooring protection. He glanced at his compass and map to further pinpoint the location. "Bea," he called over the CB set.

"Yes, Prometheus?"

"Good descent pattern for a mooring at the Port Golf Club."

"OH, GOD, LYON. NOT ANOTHER GOLF COURSE. YOU KNOW HOW THEY GET."

"It's that or the river."

Quickly calculating the average height of the golf course from his geodetic map, and keeping a careful eye on his altimeter, he turned off the propane burner and pulled the release cord for the escape of hot air. The balloon cleared the tree line at fifty feet and began to slowly settle onto the fairway of the fourteenth green. A foursome at the green turned to watch with curiosity.

Lyon tossed the mooring line overboard, but the foursome seemed immobile and made no attempt to grasp and secure the end. The balloon, still twenty-five feet above ground, was quickly covering the distance across the fairway toward a line of transmission cables. Lyon pulled the ripping panel. Great quantities of air escaped in a rush and the balloon sank inward as it settled rapidly to the ground.

The basket hit a sand trap with a jolt, and Lyon tumbled out as quickly as he could to fasten the mooring line, as a safety precaution, to the nearest tree. The balloon bag settled to the ground, the large Wobbly face turning inward as it enveloped the basket.

"Hey, you!" a voice from behind him said.

Lyon turned to see a heavy-set man waving a number five iron at him. "Yes?"

"Would you move that Goddamn thing so I can play through?"

Purple fog surrounded the house on the Green, and he knew that wasn't right, for the house was white with black shutters. He beat at the fog as it swirled behind and around him, but it wouldn't leave and he started toward the door as people yelled behind him.

He was outside again, feet straddling the front

41

RICHARD FORREST

wheel as he firmly held the handlebars and she
climbed onto the black seat. "Don't worry, Daddy. I
can do it," she said, and he turned and went into the
house on the Green.

Lyon awoke with a start, perspiration beading his
forehead. Sleep gone, the images of the nightmare dissipated slowly. He wished he smoked so he could
have a cigarette.

The day she died he had walked from the house on
the Green and never returned. On the following morning he resigned his teaching position at the College.
The first book had been for her, and it had helped,
and the pain had become at least bearable. Finally,
they had found Nutmeg Hill and renovated it, and yet
even today Lyon avoided the Green whenever he
could.

It had taken Rocco Herbert three weeks to find the
driver of the car. Someone at City Hall had told Lyon
that the big police officer had contacted every body
shop in the state, working eighteen hours a day until
he found the hit-and-run driver.

"ANSWER THE PHONE, PLEASE." Bea's voice dragged
him back and he sleepily reached for the bedside
phone.

"The cat chewed Remley's Wobbly, and she wants
to know if you could get her another one."

"Oh, God, Rocco. It's two o'clock in the morning."

"She made me promise to call you."

"She shouldn't be up so late."

"She went to bed at seven, but I wanted to get the
chemist's report on the metal assay before I called
you. I had them work through and call me as soon as
it was done."

42

"I would have thought a crime that had waited thirty years to be discovered could wait until morning to be solved."

"I took it down verbatim, just as they gave it to me."

"Go ahead," Lyon said.

"O.K. I just hope you know what they're talking about. Here it is. The specimen submitted weighed point seven one four six grams. X-ray and spectograph tests were performed and correlated with the other tests indicated below with a resulting correlation to prove accuracy. A Gooch silver run showed a percentage of silver and . . ."

"Never mind all that," Lyon said. "Is there any palladium content?"

"Palladium? No, none. What does that mean?"

"It probably means that our adult male victim was either European or else someone who liked to get his dental work done in the old country."

"Where in hell did you pick that up?"

"Three years ago when I had my front teeth capped, nothing to read except my dentist's library. We've been using palladium in dental work since the early thirties; European dentistry didn't start until after the war."

"That might help." The Chief's voice was interested and contemplative. "Maybe Immigration can help us, although I'm not quite sure how."

"Let's think about it. See you tomorrow."

Lyon hung up and rolled over in bed. After ten minutes he realized that the attempt was useless. Sleep was gone, and he went downstairs to the study to see what machinations he might invent for his precocious cat.

"You're not going to cut my balls off!"

The prospective gubernatorial candidate stood by the fireplace shaking his finger vehemently at Beatrice.

"I am not recommending that," she replied. "I don't advocate cutting, chopping, or in any way amputating any part of man's anatomy. I just say our platform should include encouragement for vasectomy clinics and information centers."

"I've had twelve children and might have twelve more." The ice clinked in the candidate's glass and sloshed liquor over onto the hearth.

"You didn't have them. YOUR WIFE DID." Beatrice had lost control of her voice again and the candidate looked startled.

"Some call that genocide of the blacks," the black attorney in the corner of the room said and looked startled to be in agreement, for the first time, with the candidate.

"I'M GOING TO GIVE YOU A LESSON IN MALE PLUMBING," Beatrice told the candidate in her usual tone.

"Don't you yell at me, Senator."

Lyon Wentworth slipped out the french doors onto the patio as his wife, followed by a phalanx of other women, stalked the candidate.

The other party noises subsided, the various conversational islands giving differential preference to the dialogue by the fireplace between Bea and her opponent. Lyon shut the patio door behind him, cutting

44

off all but the slightest murmur of the argument. He swished the ice in his drink and drained half the glass.

At the edge of the patio a small parapet ran the length of the rear of the house, and he stood, one foot on the edge, looking off toward the river.

"You're a quiet one," the voice behind him said.

He turned to see Martha Herbert. "Hi. Not really, it's just that I'm afraid that the politicians have taken over. Where's the Chief?"

"Sulking and hiding. He saw all the politicians in there, turned white as a sheet and made a triple drink and then disappeared. He never knows when he could do himself some good. Go see him, Lyon. He should be in there socializing with those people."

"I'll talk to him," Lyon said, knowing that he would talk to Rocco, but that he certainly would not force the large man into the maelstrom now prevailing in the living room.

"Now, he's got this thing with my brother," she said vehemently.

Lyon turned toward her. Martha Herbert was a diminutive woman of barely five feet whose hair hung to her shoulders and who constantly wore demure white dresses, a little girlish idiosyncrasy that now seemed slightly ludicrous. Her head came to Rocco's shoulder, and Lyon wondered how she and Rocco ever . . . and caught the half-formed erotic thought before it completely formed. "What's this thing you're talking about?"

"His feeling about the State Police. You know, I wanted him to go into the state when he got home from the service. My brother was already a sergeant.

45

If we had all those state benefits now . . . and Rocco would probably be a captain by now too."

"He's talking about running for town clerk."

"There's no future in that. I mean, once you're town clerk, you're town clerk. There's no chief town clerk or anything . . . we'd be at a dead end."

"Yes," Lyon said. "I suppose you would." It bothered him that he didn't care for Martha Herbert very much, and he wondered how many bickering arguments his large friend had endured, although he'd never mentioned them to Lyon. "If Rocco wants to be town clerk, it might make him happy. . . ."

She tossed her hair in a contemptuous gesture. "Oh, he doesn't know what he wants. All he can say is that he's tired of giving out parking tickets, and now this business about those bodies. . . ." She grimaced.

"Can I get you another drink?"

"Yes, thank you. Scotch and water."

Lyon closed the kitchen door quietly and blocked it with his back. At the sink Beatrice was pouring ginger ale into a highball glass. She continued pouring until the foaming liquid spilled over the lip of the glass and ran over the counter into a small puddle on the floor. He went up behind her and put his hands gently on her shoulders.

She half-turned and smiled through the tears. "I blew it, Lyon. I really blew it and I don't give a damn."

He kissed the back of her neck and she sniffed through the tears. "It's all right," he whispered. "If it hadn't happened tonight it would have been some other time with that joker."

"I suppose so."

"Beatrice, there is one thing you must do."

She turned and threw her arms around his neck. "I KNOW . . . about time to have my hearing tested."

"I made an appointment for you on Tuesday."

She kissed him and he pulled her closer. "I love you," she said.

"I have an idea," he replied. "The barn; they won't miss us."

"Later. I've got to get my face repaired and go back out there and fix that bastard."

"Work against him at the state convention. Back Ed Maddaloni; he's a good man."

"Maddaloni, yes. YES." The glint returned to her eyes and she hastily brushed the remaining tears from her face. "That pompous, ignorant ass has already alienated half the people here. Let's see what I can do about the other half." With a flounce and a twitch of her rear she strode from the room, and Lyon had a picture of her adjusting her lance as she galloped onward to meet the black knight.

Lyon made drinks for Martha and Rocco and a double for himself. He went in search of the Chief.

He found Rocco Herbert at the desk in the study making aimless doodles on a yellow legal pad. He put the drink firmly in the Chief's hand.

"You didn't tell me you were going to have a God-damn political convention here," Rocco said without turning.

"I didn't know, but should have guessed. This time of year they slither under the doorway."

"Sontilly of the Hartford *Courant* is here. If he spots me he'll think I'm bucking for first selectman."

"I won't allow that. I'll tell him that the Murphys-

RICHARD FORREST

ville chief of police is in my study getting stinking drunk."

"Very funny. You know, old buddy, it's against FAA regulations to land balloons on golf courses."

"How did you know about that?"

"One of the players who you almost landed on top of is mayor down there and made a complaint to headquarters. I squelched it this time. You know, it's getting so I have to practically have a unit watching over you to keep you out of trouble. Another incident or two and you'll be barred from highway and airway."

"Thanks." Lyon picked up the large blow-ups Rocco had brought with him from the police photographers. The largest, taken from the balloon almost directly overhead, he pinned to the edge of the mantel, the edge of the photo held firmly by the feet of the Wobblies. He sat in the leather chair next to Rocco and looked at the picture.

"You've got a good camera," Rocco finally said. "Excellent clarity and detail."

They pulled on their drinks and kept looking at the aerial photograph. "You know," Lyon said, "it is too far up the hill to make sense."

"Almost on the leading edge of the ridge," Rocco replied. "Oh, man, if we were still in Korea, I'd say it would be a good spot for a company defense perimeter."

"Yes, wouldn't it," Lyon said. He took the photograph from the mantel and spread it out on the desk. Getting map dividers from his balloon navigation kit, he calculated a scale from a section of the stone wall along the road that he carefully estimated at fifty feet.

Using the dividers carefully, he made calculations on the edge of the photograph.

"What do you think you have?" Rocco asked impatiently.

Lyon tapped the pencil against his teeth and stood back from the photograph. "The grave site is 375 yards from the road, but of course that doesn't include the incline of the hill. For someone to cart three bodies through all that brush all that distance. . . . Now, look at the other side of the hill . . . right over the ridge, less than fifty yards from the grave."

Rocco squinted at the photograph, and Lyon handed him a magnifying glass. "There's a cut through there, along the edge of the ridge; it runs down through the hill on the other side of the lake."

"Right. It's an old logging road. I'll lay you ten to one that thirty years ago it was passable by auto."

"Old maps would verify that."

"Wouldn't it make a lot more sense, with three bodies, to drive a car up that way, move them a few yards and then dig the grave? Far less chance of being seen, and far more practical."

"Yes," Rocco said.

"Then what would he or she do?"

"Get the hell out of there."

"Three bodies, probably killed within minutes of each other, carried in a car or pick-up truck, near a lake . . ."

"Jesus H. Christ! The lake!"

"Drag the lake, Rocco. Let's drag that damn lake now."

*   *   *

"The secret is not to have the grappling men grapple the scuba divers," Rocco said as they stood at the edge of the lake watching the dim figures at work.

"I've got a hangover," Lyon said.

The Chief's big hand slammed into Lyon's back, almost knocking him off the bank into the lake. "There's coffee in the thermos over there. Hell, you ought to be glad I didn't take you up on starting this last night when we were both half squiffed."

"It seemed like a good idea at the time."

Lyon poured a cup of steaming black coffee from the thermos and scorched his throat as he gulped part of it. Going back to the edge of the bank, he saw Rocco bent over a large geodetic survey map. He had divided the lake into a grid system of numbered sections approximately five square yards each. Two men in each rowboat worked the edges and shallows of the lake with grappling hooks, calling back to Rocco as they finished each section. In the deeper parts divers periodically disappeared as they worked their sections.

The early day was hazy, and wraithlike tendrils of fog rose from the lake's surface. The men working the far edge of the lake were only spasmodically visible as their rowboats appeared and disappeared in lake fog.

The helmeted and goggled scuba divers rose to the surface occasionally to gesture a hand signal to Rocco which he marked down on his map.

"How long is it going to take?" Lyon asked.

Rocco shrugged cheerfully. "Who knows? An hour, maybe days."

Lyon groaned.

"You're the one who said drag the lake," Rocco said.

Lyon huddled into his coat, thankful that he'd had the foresight to bring the sheepskin jacket. Early spring mornings, particularly just after dawn, could be cold as hell. He sat down on the ground and leaned back against a tree, pulling his jacket collar high up around his face.

Rocco Herbert awakened him by kicking his insteps roughly. He blinked his eyes open and looked up at the Chief looming over him. "What is it?"

"We've found something about thirty yards down the way."

Lyon scrambled to his feet and followed the large strides of Herbert. The rowboats, about twenty yards apart, were gathered in a semi-circle off shore.

"The grapplers hit something, and I just put the divers down. We'll know in a couple of minutes if we have anything."

They stared into the opaque waters, the morning still except for occasional frog croaks and the thunk of an oar in a boat. Two helmeted scuba divers broke surface simultaneously, and one raised his hand with upturned thumb. They waded awkwardly to shore and were aided up the bank by Lyon and Rocco. With triumphant faces, they stood with dripping wetsuits and removed their mouthpieces and cowls.

"We found it, Chief. A 1938 Ford coupe."

"Good work, men," Rocco beamed.

"No, sir," the other diver said. "It's a 1938 Plymouth coupe."

"Ford," the first diver replied angrily.

"Damn it all," the second diver said. "I know an antique Plymouth when I see it."

"Ford."

"It had a hood ornament in the shape of a boat with a ring around it. I could tell that even with the rust."

"That's a Ford."

"You're out of your cotton pickin' mind," the second diver said and threw his helmet at the other's webbed feet.

"Knock it off!" Rocco bellowed.

"Yes, sir!" He snapped to attention.

"Would both you officers agree that there is a car down there, a coupe of pre-World War II vintage?"

"That's right, Chief."

"Well, then, that's just fine," Rocco continued softly. "Did we see anything else down there that we all might agree on?"

"Yes, sir. There's something else down there. Near the car, but deeper, like it went into a hole. It's longer than a car and half buried, like a wagon or some other type of vehicle."

"A caravan," Lyon said.

"No, sir," the diver said seriously. "There's no caravan, there's only one of them."

"I mean house trailer," Lyon replied. "A caravan is a house trailer."

"Yes, sir," the divers said together. "That's what it is, a house trailer."

Three

The cruiser siren missed a beat as the car hit a large hole in the logging road and skidded toward the shoulder, regained its forward momentum and screeched to a halt a few yards from Rocco and Lyon.

"Ten to one here comes the Goddamn Lone Ranger," Rocco said.

Two of the cruiser doors slammed shut simultaneously as Captain Norbert strode purposefully toward them. "We found it, Captain," the young diver said.

"Good work, men." Captain Norbert turned to Rocco and Lyon. "I told them to radio when anything significant turned up. What do we have?"

"A car and trailer," the second diver said.

"Good. Now we'll have some good hard physical evidence to work with. Chief, I imagine you are entertaining a move to request formal State Police assistance in the continuance of the investigation."

"Nope."

"Now come on, Rocco."

"Lay off, Norbert. Thanks for the help, but we'll handle the case."

"I can have derricks here in two hours; in three we'll have those vehicles on shore ready for the lab boys."

"In three you'll have a bunch of wet wreckage," Lyon said. "That stuff has been down there thirty years. The frames will have rusted through; the wood must be filled with rot; the whole damn mess will fall apart."

"We'll photo in the water and reconstruct on the land," the captain responded firmly.

"It will be a mess," Rocco agreed. "What next?"

"Let's go take a look," Lyon said.

"Dive?"

"That's the best way," Lyon replied.

"You know how?"

"Read a book once." Lyon turned to a scuba diver. "Let me borrow your stuff." The young State Police diver looked imploringly at Captain Norbert.

"His equipment is State Police property," Norbert said, and pushed the diver slightly in back of him.

"Oh, no, sir," the diver said. "I bought everything myself. I've got over a grand sunk in this stuff. The very best money can buy."

"I'm commandeering it, right now," Rocco said.

"Damn it all, Rocco. Get off your high horse," the captain said.

"We are in the confines of the incorporated Township of Murphysville. I have reason to believe a felony has been committed and that the scene of that felony is under water. I am taking this young man's equipment."

As the diver peeled off the wetsuit, Rocco and Norbert went over to a small clump of pine trees and began to argue heatedly. Lyon shivered as he removed his pants and shirt and began to pull on the wetsuit over his underwear.

"You know," the diver said, "we're never going to find a suit big enough for the Chief."

"I know," Lyon said. "I'll go down."

"I'll go with you," the diver said. "The buddy system is a necessity. I'll hold the lights for you."

"Thank you," Lyon said as the first diver jockeyed the tanks onto his shoulders and helped him adjust the straps. He donned the helmet cowl and put the mouthpiece uncomfortably into his mouth.

"You've got it in upside down," the diver said.

"Oh," Lyon replied as they helped him to adjust the mechanism. "Thank you."

As they walked slowly into the water, the police diver turned to him. "Are you sure you know what you're doing, sir?"

"Not a bit," Lyon replied. "But it doesn't look too hard."

"Thank God it's not deep," the diver said. As they reached chest-high water, the diver put his hand on Lyon's shoulder. "Wait one sec, sir. Half a lesson at least."

In three minutes he pointed out to Lyon the tank measurement indicator, the proper placement of the mouthpiece, and a few necessary items for a first shallow dive. Turning, Lyon could see Captain Norbert striding toward the shoreline in a manner too purposeful for comfort, and he quickly ducked his head under and kicked off toward deep water.

The water was illuminated in front of him for several feet, and turning he could see the police diver not far behind, carrying two large lamps. The other diver jiggled the lights and pointed downward. Twelve or fifteen feet below the surface Lyon could see the vague outline of a car and the long, rectangular roof of the trailer. They swam down and grasped the edge of the car window.

Lyon took one of the lamps from the diver and shone it through the car window. The window on the diver's side was down and he was able to signal Lyon to come over. Lyon stuck his head through the window with the lamp held before him.

Small sunfish swam between the spokes of the steering wheel, and a layer of silt rose from the floor past the level of the seats. Plants grew in the floor and sent stalk tendrils upward through the window to catch the filtered surface light.

If anything was to be found in the car, underneath the layers of silt and mud, it would have to be when it was hoisted to the surface. He backed out of the car and swung the light toward the trailer. Together they circled the long vehicle.

It had evidently dropped into a hole several feet lower than the car, and now mud and silt reached above the level of the windows, and although part of the silt, mud and plant life had been crushed away from the roof by the divers, from a short distance away the trailer would have been invisible.

Lyon put his lamp down on the trailer roof and made a hand signal to the police diver that outlined the shape of a door. The diver nodded understanding, and on the opposite side began to feel around the edge of the trailer, while Lyon started on his side. Trailer doors were almost always on the left hand side of the vehicle, to the rear, which in this case would be away from the sunken automobile.

Three feet away from the rear of the trailer, his hands deep in mud, Lyon felt the door frame. The police diver joined him and unhooked a small crowbar from his utility belt. Inserting the edge of the crowbar into the top edge of the door, they easily pried the complete door away from the frame. Lake-bottom mud slid into the trailer, but the aperture was large enough to admit them. Holding the top of the trailer, the police diver extended his feet through the doorway and with a slight shove was propelled into the vehicle. Lyon followed more slowly.

Under the circumstances the trailer's interior was in remarkable condition. It had landed easily on the soft bottom of the lake, as proven by the fact that the floor hadn't buckled. Although filled with water, the trailer's structure was sufficiently tight to keep out most forms of marine life. Trickles of silt lay in corners and around seams and window edges; but for the most part, the trailer outlined in the soft glow of the underwater lamps gave the impression of being almost habitable.

Lyon wondered about the origin of caravans and house trailers. Of course the Middle European gypsies had had them for more than two hundred years, perhaps the Visigoths before that . . . he'd have to read material on the subject.

They moved slowly through the trailer. The door entered into the main living area, with a convertible settee along the rear wall. A table fitted into the wall near the door, and beyond that a stove, cabinets and small bedroom to the front of the trailer. In the diffused light, Lyon could see that a blotchy film inundated everything in the trailer, a combination of algae and rust rising to thin knobs in certain sections, but easily wiped away.

He started with the back bedroom. A triangular-shaped object rested by the bed, and he wiped his hands across the covering growth. A peaked roof, a little window, a door, a doll house. He turned away from the tiny room with revulsion.

They opened the cabinets in the kitchen area. Food cans, still retaining their shape, but the contents unrecognizable, filled one cabinet. A set of dishes in another, and another set, oddly enough, in the final cabinet. Rusted silverware in two drawers, a gas stove with three eyes, stove ring missing from one eye.

Above the rear settee-bed was a bookcase filled with rotting books. Swimming upward, Lyon ran his hands along their spines. The books crumpled and disintegrated before him and pieces of pulp floated before his eyes. At the end of the shelf he found a large volume bound in calfskin and gently removed it. The print was unreadable and fell from his touch, but he could make out one word of the title on the spine, "Das . . ."

The police diver grasped Lyon's shoulder and gestured to their air gauges. Only a few minutes left. They swam through the trailer and together, at the bottom of the clothes cabinet, dragged out a large tool-box. The police diver pried the lip open with his crowbar and they looked into the rusted contents. The tools were alien to Lyon, rusted metal in odd shapes and forms. He picked up one small piece, a gauge of some sort, but its readings were rusted through, and he let it fall back into the box.

Gesturing to the police diver to continue the search, he let himself float free. His back came to rest against the trailer roof, giving him a draftsman's view of the trailer as he bobbed gently. There must be a pattern, an indication of life style in the things he had just seen that would fit together to form a living picture of the people who had lived here. There was not the slightest doubt that this was the house trailer of the three victims found on the ridge. The room of a little girl, the remains of artifacts and clothing belonging to a man and woman; obviously three people lived here. A man, wife and child. Now, what else . . . Lyon Wentworth had a great deal of thinking to do.

Why was Rocco Herbert standing waist deep in lake water with all his clothes on? Why was Rocco holding him by the back while other troopers carried him to shore?

They laid Lyon on the bank and began to strip off the diving equipment and wetsuit. Large hands wrapped him in a blanket. A few feet away, near a pine, the police diver bent over and retched.

Captain Norbert was yelling at Chief Herbert, which somehow, Lyon thought, seemed to be the natural order of things.

"If he had died my ass would be in a sling, damn it!" the captain said.

"He didn't die, Captain," Rocco's quiet voice returned. "The guy's got a charmed life."

"No more. No more dives except to attach the cables. We're hauling the whole mess up."

"All right, for Christ's sake." Rocco left the captain and bent over Lyon with a plastic cup. "Brandy. Good for what ails you."

Lyon drank greedily, feeling the warmth spread to his feet. "That is good. What happened?"

"You bastard," the big man's quiet voice said. "You

are now officially a menace on land, sea and air. Not only did you almost drown, but that young trooper almost bought it bringing you out. What in God's name were you doing down there?"

"Doing? Why, thinking."

"Thinking. Jesus Christ! If the kid hadn't been an expert diver, you'd be thinking for eternity. Your tanks were out."

By early afternoon the equipment was assembled along the edge of the lake. Lyon and Rocco had gone off to a nearby diner for a large breakfast and home for a change of clothes. They returned in time to see the last traces of activity before the hoist began the raising of the vehicles.

The automobile came up first, water and mud streaming through the windows and doorway as it swiveled across the water and was set down gently on a flatbed truck.

"If that's not a thirty-eight Ford, I'll eat it," Lyon's savior exclaimed in glee as he rushed to examine the car. He turned back to Rocco in amazement. "Hey, Chief. There's no engine in this thing."

"And I'll bet no body serial numbers either," Rocco said.

"I didn't think he'd leave the marker plates on," Lyon said.

"Scratch that one off."

In short order the roof of the trailer broke through the surface of the lake. Captain Norbert gave a quick, triumphant glance over his shoulder toward Rocco and Lyon, and directed his gaze forward in time to see the trailer break neatly in two.

It hung from the guy wires for a suspended moment, each half gaping downward as silt, furniture and myriad other material slid into the lake. Then the remainder of the frame crumpled, and in seconds the trailer was in pieces, the debris falling into the water to sink almost immediately.

Captain Norbert turned back to them. "We'll dredge the whole lake if we have to; we'll get every piece . . . eventually."

The office of the Murphysville police chief was next to the two detaining cells, just over the first selectman's office and in front of the library. Lyon and Rocco sat in straight wooden chairs, their feet on the radiator, finishing the brandy and silently contemplating the erection of a hamburger palace across the street that violated the Village Green.

The phone rang and Rocco picked it up impatiently. He listened. "Yes, Mrs. Henderson, but I've been out to your place three times this week already. The court says he can't come out there except on the children's visiting days. . . . I know, yes. . . . Well, if you let him in the bed, it's up to you to get him out of the bed." He hung up with a bang. "She'll call the first selectman about that and I'll have to go out there."

"Lock them both up."

"I would, except they'd screw in the detaining cell and embarrass the drunks."

Rocco flipped the now empty brandy bottle into the trash can. "Couldn't you do the dredging yourself, or with town maintenance people?" Lyon asked.

"Not enough men or equipment for it. Norbert has

the upper hand. It'll take him days to get all that stuff from the bottom and sort through it, but he'll do it; he's very thorough. If only I could have gone down there myself, or if you could have made another dive or two instead of . . . thinking."

Lyon's feet came off the radiator with a bang as the front legs of the chair hit the floor. He crossed to Rocco's desk, scratched around for a pad and pencil and made a few notes.

"Let's see what we have. Probabilities, that's all. One. Three people inhabited the trailer; two adults, man and woman, and a child. It was probably owned by our victims. No license plates on trailer or car."

"I'd be greatly surprised if any serial numbers whatsoever are found."

"I think you're right," Lyon said. "Let's see what else. They were Jewish, of course."

Rocco's chair came down with a thud as he turned to Lyon excitedly. "How come?"

"Two sets of dishes. Two what seemed to be complete and separate sets. I suppose you can keep a kosher trailer as well as home."

"Jesus H. Christ, go on."

"Part of a book title, the only part I could read, Das."

"Das is goot."

"Exactly. German."

Rocco began to pace the small room. "Anything else? Anything we can put a handle on?"

"The tool-box. It was corroded as hell and didn't seem to have the usual things like hammers and screw drivers. I got a close look at one gauge but couldn't make it out because of its condition."

"What did it look like?"

Lyon made a pencil sketch of the implement he had held in his hand for a few moments under water. Rocco took the drawing and turned it in several directions. "I can't make it out," Lyon said.

"It's a micrometer," Rocco said.

"A micrometer. Yes, a machinist's tool. A tool and diemaker's box."

"It's a possible."

"A probable."

Lyon put his feet on the desk and closed his eyes. "Now what do we have? A family of three are murdered; no one files a missing persons report. Probably because there are no relatives in this country. We have to work on the assumption that because of the teeth and the book title, at least the father was of European origin. They were Jewish, kept a kosher home, and the father was either a machinist or tool and diemaker. Since they died during the war, he probably worked at one of the plants or machine shops in the Greater Hartford area."

"They could have been from out of state," Rocco said. "Passing through as tourists . . . on their way to and from anywhere."

"Unlikely. During World War II there was gas rationing, little pleasure driving, and a housing shortage. A time when people would be glad to have a trailer to live in."

"Do you know how many machinists and tool and diemakers there are in Connecticut, and of Jewish descent, and how many there are or might have been in thirty years?"

"Hardly a lead," Lyon replied. "Yet, let's assume that at least the man emigrated here from Germany. Because of his age, let's assume that he left Germany sometime after the Nurbenberg Laws."

"What are they?"

"The Nazi passed them in September 1935; in essence they declared all Jews non-persons. The war started in 1938. That's only a three-year period. We also think he was either a machinist or tool and die-maker, or perhaps an engineer."

Rocco looked depressed, his jubilation of moments ago now completely dissipated. "There would be thousands of German mechanics who came over here during that period."

"Unfortunately for them, not as many as you'd think. What we're interested in are the permanent resident cards of those who came to Connecticut."

"Damn it all, Lyon, you're still too complicated. It's an impossible job to track down."

"Wait a minute. Think about the pathologist's report. The adult male was around five foot three, age between 30 and 35. Now what are we looking for?"

Rocco beamed. "Emigrated here between 1935 and 1938 from Germany, to Connecticut, with a probable occupation."

"Adult male, age between 20 and 26 during those years, height and build we have, state of destination we have, occupation is narrowed."

"And until he gained citizenship, if he did, he'd have to register once a year."

"Can you do it?" Lyon asked.

"You're Goddamn right I can do it! With this kind of

data I can run it through Washington as an official request. I'll have it in days."

"You had better make it faster than that," Lyon said. "Once your brother-in-law gets through that mud he won't be far behind us."

"that's the most ridiculous supposition i've heard since they wanted to nominate my friend big daddy for governor. it's all conjecture."

"Will you adjust your hearing aid?"

"What?"

"Turn it up."

"Oh, all right." Bea reached for her ear only to look blank. "I'm not wearing it."

"Lower your voice; you're disturbing the other diners."

She looked rather sheepishly around the room and then back to Lyon. "It is ridiculous, you know. You hardly have a fact to go on."

"I prefer to think of it as a probability. We'll know soon. Rocco thinks we'll have the first reports from Immigration tomorrow."

The restaurant was an old train terminal. Outside, a dining car on the unused track acted as cocktail lounge. The high roof and windows gave a more spacious aura to the room than it warranted. The waiter set the escargots before them, and Lyon sipped on his martini, Bea on her Manhattan.

"Even if you find out who they are, what then?" Bea asked.

"As Rocco said, you can't begin to find a murderer unless you at least know who the victims are."

"Aren't most mass killings, killings of whole families, done by madmen?" Bea asked.

He smiled across the table at her. "And madwomen, or, if you prefer, madperson."

"Touché. But isn't that usually the case?"

"Unfortunately, at least from my readings; but isn't anyone who knocks people off nuts? Slightly less nuts when they go to the extreme care our murderer went to . . . buried bodies, hidden cars and trailers, engines removed . . . there's a macabre rationale to that." They grasped the snail shells with .tongs and gently extricated the meat with small forks. "This is great garlic sauce," Lyon said.

"Never could eat snails," the voice behind them said.

They turned to see Senator Marcuse, state minority leader, beaming through his carefully cultivated moustache. Well-tailored, even in early spring his face deeply tanned and healthy. A man who many spoke of as a possible future state chairman, but unfortunately not a potential candidate for the national scene because of a facial tic that proved unfortunate on any television appearance.

"I heard . . . saw you from across the room and just thought I'd say hello."

"You know my husband, Lyon, I believe," Bea said.

They shook hands, and Lyon winced slightly at the heavy grip of the minority leader.

"Yes, we've met," Lyon replied.

"Sorry I couldn't make the party Saturday, but I had a speech." The politician's cheek twitched, and

Lyon wondered what that meant. "Oh, just one thing, Beatrice. Murphysville is in your district, isn't it?"

Lyon and Beatrice knew as well as the minority leader did that not only was it in Beatrice's district, but they lived in Murphysville. "Yes, it is," Bea replied, leaning forward in an attempt to hear every word.

"If you get a chance Monday, I wonder if you'd talk to the chief of police down there. The State Police commissioner called me this morning about some flap on those three bodies they discovered. You know how it is—the local constabulary isn't in any position to handle an investigation of that magnitude. Have them officially request state intervention."

"I'll see what I can do," Bea replied.

With a wave the minority leader left the table. They watched him weave his way around the intervening tables, stopping twice to speak briefly to other diners before rejoining his wife. They sat quietly and Lyon ordered another martini for himself. Beatrice twirled the cherry in her half-empty drink.

"Thanks for the support," he said.

"I just said I'd see what I could do. There's no real problem until the Governor calls me in, and I won't get that for a while."

"How in the hell do you suppose he found out we were going to eat here tonight?"

"Darling, you're supposed to know those things. You tell me."

The Chateaubriand arrived on the serving wagon and they watched as the captain began to carve it with a flourish.

* * *

Kimberly stood with her back against the refrigerator door, her brown arms folded defiantly beneath her large breasts, her Afro high above the belligerent eyes defying Lyon.

"The Man doesn't get food from this chick," she said.

"Damn it all, Kim. All we want is a chicken sandwich and a bottle of beer."

"Then you go into the fields, wring the neck of a chicken, pluck and cook him. No Fascist pigs are eating here."

"He is not a Fascist pig. Now cut it out."

"Let him go to the diner on the highway and eat free like the other pigs do," she yelled.

"God damn it, Kim! Rocco is my oldest friend."

"That's your problem, bourgeois pig."

"Look at it this way. Join us for lunch, overhear the oppressive tactics we're plotting, and then you can report back to your leader."

She contemplated this for a moment and then her eyes twinkled. "You manipulate and exploit me."

"Absolutely," Lyon said.

"You pay me slave wages, hold me in bondage and take advantage of me."

"Of course we do. But damn it, we're hungry."

She moved away and opened the refrigerator door. "You'll get yours one day," she said, taking a chicken from the refrigerator. She put the cooked chicken on the cutting-board and brought the cleaver down across the breastbone with a guillotinelike whack. Lyon returned to the study to rejoin Rocco Herbert.

Kimberly had come to Nutmeg Hill a year ago as

leader of a militant group of welfare mothers. They had picketed, Kimberly with a bull-horn that spewed forth revolutionary slogans and demands that Beatrice, chairman of the welfare legislation committee, resign. Beatrice and Lyon had placed a card table in the driveway circle, loading it with heaping platters of roast beef sandwiches and coffee. For an hour the women continued their march, ignoring the waiting couple, and Kimberly's voice had grown hoarse as she raised her tirade against the "oppressors."

With a shrug, Beatrice had gone over to the large black woman to talk in a low voice. Perhaps the futility of the isolated protest march was the final weighing factor, since the nearest neighbor was a half mile away and no television or radio people were in attendance. While Bea and Kim argued, the rest of the women joined Lyon for lunch.

As a brisk autumn wind chilled them, protesters and Wentworths had gone into the house, where Kimberly and Beatrice spent the remainder of the afternoon in loud and acrimonious argument.

The welfare mothers had left in a minibus at four, and at five Lyon served cocktails to the still-talking Bea and Kim. As the evening progressed each woman made concessions to the other, a strange bond was created between the two women, an unusual relationship between one born of patrician New England stock and the vibrant young black woman from the ghetto.

Kimberly had stayed the night and on the following day moved her possessions and daughter into the garage apartment near the house. At first she started as an unpaid assistant to Bea's committee, and that expanded to an interim state appointment when the legislature was in session. Now her position was inviolate as aide to Bea, research assistant to Lyon, overseer of the house, and in the ensuing year an invaluable help, and she finally agreed to accept a salary.

They lost Kim for several days a year as she disappeared to distant cities to organize protests, or to speak at meetings; and now her little daughter was entering the seventh grade and losing interest in Lyon's brand of monster as she became increasingly aware of real-life boys.

Lyon and Rocco looked down at the montage of intense, serious young Jewish men on the floor. The faces that stared from the small photographs on the permanent resident cards were gaunt with brooding darkness.

"Christ," Rocco said. "They look like prison mug shots."

"In a way that's what they are," Lyon said. "God only knows what they went through to get here."

The search by the immigration authorities and the Federal Bureau of Investigation had turned up sixteen names with sixteen photographs and visa information. Sixteen names of Jewish males emigrating from Germany or of German origin as they made circuitous routes to this country. Each had arrived between 1935 and 1938 and was approximately five foot three inches tall, with some sort of machinist or engineering background. Each had moved to Connecticut, and each was now lost to the authorities because of death, failure to register, formal citizenship or other factors. Of the thousand possible names they were down to sixteen.

"It's still going to be a hell of a lot of work," Rocco said.

Lyon thought for a moment. Some of the names had known addresses in the forties, others had dossiers that ended in the late thirties. He knew there were other sources they could go to, the Social Security Administration, the Armed Forces, or other governmental agencies that became involved in every person's life.

"You know, Rocco, it makes you realize how impossible it is to disappear completely. There are too many bureaucratic tracks on each of us."

"Still, Connecticut is a big state for a little state," Rocco said, "and thirty years is a long time. Where in hell do we start?"

"We'll go on the assumption that the man we're looking for lived somewhere in the Greater Hartford area, say in a thirty-mile radius. Let's start with the State Bureau of Vital Statistics and see if we can pick up the deaths from our group."

Rocco's hand already cradled the phone and he dialed the Bureau of Vital Statistics. In twenty minutes they'd given the names and received a reply. "Thank you very much," Rocco said. "As a double check I'll duplicate the request by mail." He turned to Lyon and handed him a pad with a neatly aligned list of names. Four had been crossed off with the notation, "deceased."

"And then there were twelve," Lyon said.

Kimberly kicked the door open and slammed two plates of sandwiches on the desk. "Off you, pig," she said to Rocco.

"Kimberly, have I told you recently how much I love you?" Rocco said.

"Go to hell, man," she replied and strode from the room.

"Someday, Lyon, will you tell her that I don't oppress ghetto dwellers—that Murphysville doesn't even have a ghetto?"

"I told her," Lyon said. "But she said that if Murphysville did have a ghetto you would oppress them."

The big man shrugged and they went back to the lists. "Well," Rocco said, "let's see who on this list is alive and kicking."

They drew a thirty-mile circle on a road map, using the grave site as the center. They found that the ring included in its area a total of twenty-two towns. They decided that the quickest initial check would be through the phone company.

Two hours later they had marked seven more names off their lists. Personal calls to the seven, either at home or at their place of business, verified that they were in fact the emigrants staring so solemnly from the old visa photographs.

"Jesus," Rocco said. "Five left. They could be anywhere."

"Let's try the school systems in the area. They keep records," Lyon said. "Let's find out if any of the names left had a daughter in school during 1943 in the seven to ten age range."

As a small boy Lyon could remember driving through the cities and towns in the area encompassed within their circle. His father, a doctor, often traveled to what were then remote areas. At that time, as throughout the country, what were now thriving suburban towns and cities were still sleepy hamlets. An immigrant settling in the area, and likely working in a factory or foundry, would probably live in a metropolitan area near his place of work and not too distant from fellow immigrants. At that time, the North End of Hartford held the Jewish ghetto. Although the murdered family lived in a trailer, he thought it unlikely they would have moved far from the city.

They were lucky on the first call to the Hartford Board of Education. The impatient clerk, after rummaging through old records, gave them a verification of two of their names. Each had a child in the public school system in the early 1940s; each of the girls was of the proper age.

They made an appointment to see the records on the following morning.

Lyon sat in the police cruiser in front of the post office while Rocco Herbert wrote out two tickets for overtime parking. When the large man finally heaved himself behind the wheel with a satisfied grin, Lyon turned to him impatiently.

"Overtime parking, when we're trying to find a murderer?"

"That's a fifteen-minute zone by the post office, and I know damn well they've been there for over an hour."

"We've got an appointment at the Board of Ed."

Rocco shrugged. "I know. Too many years, too many parking tickets. It's become a thing." He threw the car in gear and they started toward the highway.

Near the entrance to the Interstate a housewife in a station wagon filled with children ran a stop sign. The cruiser began to slow until Lyon put his arm on Rocco's.

"I know. I can't help it," Rocco said.

"I hate to see crime run rampant in Murphysville for a whole morning, Rocco, but . . ."

"All right, wise guy," the big man replied. "See how you'd fare if you'd been doing the same thing for twenty years and then . . . say in your case, if you had to write a book with more than two syllable words."

"Touché."

The neat blue badge with white lettering read, "Miss Louella Parsons." The wearer of the badge, a gaunt, white-haired woman in her sixties, stood defiantly at the counter, separating her protected school records from the remainder of the world. "It is immaterial to me what they told you in the front office," she said. "These records are only available to certain persons on written request."

"This is a police matter, lady."

"That patch on your sleeve says Murphysville, not Hartford."

"We try to cooperate with all local authorities," Rocco said, impatience edging his voice.

"I suggest you get authorization from the local police," she replied.

"Louella Parsons," Rocco said, authority ringing his voice. "That name's familiar to me. I bet you have unpaid parking tickets in Murphysville. Right, lady?"

She stepped back from the counter. "I don't even drive."

"Jaywalking then."

"Wait a minute," Lyon said softly. "Louella Parsons was a movie gossip columnist, Hearst syndicate, I believe."

"No relation," Miss Parsons said primly.

"It might help if I explained why we're here," Lyon said. In quick strokes he painted her a picture of the grave site and briefly sketched their investigation so far, and their hope that the file of one of the two girls might give them a lead to the identity of the victims.

In a few minutes they were sitting at a small table in the well-protected sanctity of Miss Parsons' record room. Each held a folder in his hands while Miss Parsons stood nearby, part instructor and part protector of the realm.

The serious eight-year-old eyes of Rebecca Meyerson stared out solemnly at Lyon. The corners of the lips seemed slightly stretched as if smothering a smile and fighting to maintain composure. A black-haired girl with raven eyes and alabaster skin. As Lyon closed the folder he could imagine the little girl jumping from the photographer's chair to skip down the hall to class. He knew with a start that if this was the victim, that if this little girl was the one whose body . . .

"What's in yours?" Rocco asked.

"Oh, it's not this one," Miss Parsons said, snatching the folder from Lyon. "There's a note on the outside of the folder that the family moved to California."

"Where did the father work?" Rocco asked.

Miss Parsons efficiently flipped open the folder. "Father, Meyer Meyerson, address 1215 Houston Blvd., employed at the Houston Company."

"But moved to California," Lyon said with relief.

"We've got it here, then," Rocco said jubilantly. "Want to see her picture?" he said, and handed the folder across the table to Lyon.

"No, thank you. Are you sure it's her?"

"Got to be. Listen. Father, Moshe Eisenberg, home address 210 Asylum, place of business, Pratt and Whitney Aircraft."

"210 Asylum. That's the Civic Center."

"Sure it is, now. But we've got something to go on. We'll track them down."

As they left Miss Parsons, Rocco thumped Lyon on the back, and Lyon was grateful that he hadn't looked at the Eisenberg girl's photo.

The young and efficient assistant personnel manager at the aircraft plant was most helpful as she ushered them into a private conference room. She sat at the end of the table, with pencil poised. Long red hair framed her youthful face.

They quickly told her the story, and her intense young face became even more intense. "Of course," she said. "He could have worked here or at one of the other plants, but let's start here." She jumped from her seat and scurried from the room, only to return in a few minutes with a personnel folder and a puzzled look.

"You have his folder?" Lyon asked.

"Yes," she replied. "I have Moshe Eisenberg's folder, but it's very strange. The folder just ends. I mean, it's like there should be other pages or something, but it just ends in 1943." She paused to reflect a moment. "That was during World War II or something, wasn't it?"

"Or something," Lyon said and felt old.

"Record keeping wasn't the best then. Lots of men were in and out of here, but this folder just ends . . . doesn't say if he was terminated or anything."

Lyon and Rocco glanced across the table at each other with the knowledge that they now had an address turned into a civic center and a file that just ended.

"I just don't understand it," the young personnel assistant said. "We try to be so careful, but of course we never have to go back this far in the records unless someone is still here." She tapped her pencil with a click against the table. "You know what we might do. This man was in Department 210. Just yesterday I was processing a retirement for the superintendent of that department. He's been here over thirty years and just might remember something."

Department 210 was a die shop almost a quarter of a mile through the plant from the executive offices. They followed the clicking heels of the young girl, and since conversation was difficult in the din of the factory, Lyon glanced at Rocco and saw that he was intent on the taut skirt of the young woman in front of them. Lyon nudged him in the ribs and the large man looked over at him with a grin and proceeded to inspect the overhead crane system with great intensity.

The superintendent of Department 210 was wearing safety goggles and bending over a lathe as he helped the operator to set up the machine. He turned quickly and smiled at the young personnel assistant, then beckoned them toward a small glass-enclosed office.

"These gentlemen are trying to locate a Moshe Eisenberg who worked in this department a number of years ago," she said. "It's very strange, the personnel records just end . . . nothing . . . no notations, nothing. We thought you might remember something about the man."

The superintendent looked at them blankly for a moment and then slowly removed his goggles and laid them neatly on the desk. "Why do you want him?" he asked.

"We think he may have been murdered," Rocco answered.

"Moshe Eisenberg?"

"That's what we think."

The superintendent blinked and then began to laugh until he grasped the edge of the desk with both hands. "Well," he choked. "Well, then, I guess I killed him. I'm Moshe Eisenberg. Changed my name to Monte Eisenhower in 1943. Seemed like the patriotic thing to do at the time."

Four

Since getting drunk at eleven in the morning seemed slightly obscene, Rocco left Lyon off at Nutmeg Hill and proceeded back to Murphysville to wreak utter devastation on overtime parkers and those who pass stopped school buses.

The Wobblies grinned at Lyon from the mantelpiece, and Kimberly, sneakered feet on desk and phone in hand, was arranging a protest meeting for the Attica brothers.

Lyon stomped out onto the patio and contemplated the blossoming trees and nesting birds. Contemplating trees and birds is a hell of a thing to do if that's not what you want to do, he thought. Going back into the study, he glared at Kim, who waved him away with an obscene gesture.

In the kitchen he made himself a dreadful cup of instant coffee and sulked at the formica-topped table. He ran the tips of his fingers over the haphazard design of the table top. Formless, erratic, purposeless . . .

Lyon Wentworth was angry with himself. Angry for his initial involvement with this case in the first place, angry for looking at the grave and for deluding Rocco into thinking that an amateur and a small town police chief could best the power of one of the most highly trained State Police forces in the country.

His theory of the identification of the male victim had seemed rational, to fit the scanty clues available.

79

Now there were three choices available: one, to chuck
the whole thing and go back to his book; two, to re-
think the whole matter and try to come up with something else; or three, continue to pursue the same path
with the . . . with the realization that if the murders
were not done by a madman, all possible attempts
would have been made to cover up identity. In retrospect it had to be considered that the murderer so far
had done a pretty damn good job in covering up
leads.

What other avenues were open? The murder
weapon? Considering what Rocco had told him of the
pathologist's report and what he'd seen in the trailer,
Lyon suspected it was the missing stove ring. Even
locating that wouldn't prove much. The ownership of
the land and lake where the trailer was found was a
dead end; the corporate face of the Water Company
had yielded nothing. Reluctant liaison by Rocco with
his brother-in-law of the State Police had produced no
further results. The dredging operation was now almost complete and, except for finding thousands of
pieces of ancient trailer, had turned up nothing tangible.

If it had only been one of the two little girls whose
records they'd looked at . . . but the evidence was
undeniable. Monty-Moshe was quite obviously alive,
with a 37-year-old daughter living in Fresno, California, and little Rebecca was also living in California,
according to . . .

Something was wrong. He realized that he'd been
denying the subconscious premonition that had been
with him for hours. He had fought it, submerged it
back into his mind, obliterated it because he had

willed it so, because he refused to consider the possibility, because he didn't want it to be Rebecca.

He went back into the study to find Kimberly still intent on the telephone. During a break in her conversation he spoke loudly. "The FBI's at the back door and respectfully wishes to interview you about certain of your activities."

Kimberly slammed the phone down. "Are those mothers back again . . ." She stalked out as Lyon gratefully reached for the still warm phone.

Miss Louella Parsons sounded disarmingly young on the phone, and it took will to conjure up her rather waspish face and manner. He asked that she get Rebecca Meyerson's folder.

As he waited for her to return to the phone, Kimberly stuck her head in the doorway. "There's no one out there," she yelled.

"They're probably digging up the pasture for hidden arms," he replied.

Miss Parsons came back on the phone. "I have the file. Exactly what did you want to know, Mr. Wentworth?"

"I'm interested in the notation that the family moved to California."

"Yes. The local school probably made it after a call from a member of the family, or a truant officer's report when the child never returned to school. It could have happened any number of ways."

"Wouldn't the file show the shipment of records to the new school?"

There was a pause on the line, then the return of the now doubtful voice. "That is strange. Under ordinary circumstances a transcript would have been sent along, or sent when the new school requested it. Of course, that form could have been lost from the file years ago."

"But under ordinary circumstances there should have been a further notation, a follow-up."

"Yes, usually there would be."

"Thank you very much." Lyon Wentworth hung up with a sick feeling, the photograph of the dark-haired girl clear in his mind. He quickly dialed town police headquarters and asked for Chief Herbert. "How's it going?" he asked when Rocco picked up.

"Just great, really great. Fourteen parking tickets in an hour, which is my record. Caught a selectman and a member of the Board of Ed."

"You'll get in trouble doing that."

"I'm not stupid. I scribble a signature on the ticket, and when they complain I blame it on a new man. Now I'm going over patrolmen's time sheets to see if I can suspend anyone for anything. As you can tell, I'm in a good mood." His voice lowered. "I've got to call in the state, Lyon."

"Wait another day. I may have something."

"Another day." He could sense the Chief's voice attempting to sound not too hopeful. "You really think you have something?"

"I guess so, Rocco. At least I think I guess so. I'll let you know this time tomorrow."

"Call me as soon as you can."

Houston Boulevard had changed since he was a boy. The Park River had flowed green and was filled with shad. Now the river was cement-covered and ran murky in hidden culverts, while the whole area was covered with clusters of elevated portions of Interstate highway. The Houston Company had grown over the years until now it was one of the largest factories in the area.

He pulled the car to a stop in front of the address the school records had indicated and beat the steering wheel in disappointment. The address, next to the Houston factory, was the General Douglas MacArthur housing development, one of the first large city projects built in the early fifties. Before him in drab alignment stretched endless rows of dull brick buildings with parking lots filled with vintage cars.

He grimaced at the artistic development of man. After all, it took great talent and ingenuity, one had to really work at it in order to take a perfectly pleasant area and turn it into a shambles, a shambles where people lived. He started the car and eased it down the street wondering why other nations seemed to do so much better with their housing projects than this country.

The Houston Company was completely surrounded by a high chain link fence. The entrance to the large parking lot was guarded by a sentrylike building with a movable lift gate. The gray-haired and uniformed guard at the gate handed Lyon a visitor's pass, pointed to the executive offices, and let him pass.

Lyon had to shake his head and remind himself that he was in another factory miles away from the aircraft plant. The young personnel assistant was practically the twin sister of the one at the other plant. Her young, intense face turned toward him with great interest as she seriously considered the problem. She left him in the small office and returned in minutes.

"I'm terribly sorry, Mr. Wentworth. Our employment records prior to 1950, except for the men still working here, have all been destroyed. There have been so many here, our files would be voluminous, and it does cost two dollars a year per linear foot of storage. So, you can . . ."

He rose tiredly. "Thank you, I appreciate your looking." On an impulse as he left the Houston Company he stopped at the gate and called to the security guard. "Have you worked here long?"

"About twelve years," the guard replied.

"Oh, then you came in the early sixties."

"Right, 1961 to be exact. But I know the area pretty well, let me tell you. Used to patrol here when I was on the force."

"Is that right?"

"Yep. Twenty years with the Hartford P.O."

"Do you remember what was on that property before the housing development was built?"

"Sure do. The company owned it. Used it for temporary housing during the war. Hell, the company was hiring people by the car load and there weren't no place to put them. They had quonset huts and things like that."

"That's interesting. What about trailers?"

"Sure. There must have been a hundred trailers over there in the forties."

"Are you sure?"

"Of course I'm sure."

"Thanks. Really, thanks a lot."

The guard saluted as he drove off.

* * *

The gentle brush of warmth from cheek to folded fingers was the only measurement of time Rabbi Ben Alchium now knew. "Ten to two," a lilting voice on the porch told him as she tucked the blanket around his legs and folded his hands. He did not believe her, for he knew that a lifetime had passed while the sun, ever so slowly, moved from cheek to finger.

At first there was always the city of Pinsk, and he was young, and often ran sideways as children do. He could not remember the game. The child that was himself laughed, jumped and ran while others were there in the sun also. Somehow the details of the game itself were never clear. His father, a teacher also, forbidding behind the long beard, and yet often holding him tightly until the bad times came and the sun moved on.

Hours of study in a warm room where a dark girl laughed. He knew it was his wife, but now she was gone, and the sun moved on.

There were children, and children of children and more, and often he wasn't sure which were which, for he was very old. As the sun warmed his fingers he stood before the group. The raven-haired girl looking toward him while the children were there with the others, and his voice was strong as he spoke, and that was his life, and as the sun moved on he lived it each day.

The light hand on his shoulder interrupted, and that was wrong, for the sun was not yet gone. "There's someone to see you."

A chair scraped, and he sensed a man near him, perhaps a child of a child, and he turned to look.

"Rabbi Alchium."

"Yes."

"I need your help," Lyon said.

"What can I do for you?"

"A man, a great many years ago, a member of your temple perhaps."

"There were so many, it is hard to remember." The hand turned the chair and the sun fell on his cheek again and a child laughed and ran sideways in Pinsk. "I wonder what game we played?" the Rabbi said.

"Pardon, sir?" Lyon asked.

"Nothing," the Rabbi replied. "What about the man from my temple?"

Lyon leaned forward. "He was named Meyerson. In 1943 he was a tool maker or an engineer, married, with a little girl. He kept an orthodox home."

"Yes, many did then. Now, even the children of the children do not. There were many Meyersons. So many, they all become one."

"This Meyerson left one day, without a farewell, without any word, and no one ever heard of him again."

The Rabbi leaned back and the sun was gone. He remembered such a Meyerson, and the hurt had been great. "Yes," he said. "I remember such a man," and there was a tear in his eye. "A faithful member of the Minyon each morning, a strong faithful man and a friend; and he left without a word."

"You do remember him."

"Yes, I must have failed him greatly. I went to where he lived, his house that moved."

"A trailer."

"Yes. And it was gone. Without a word to the temple, and someone said he moved away. I failed him."

Lyon Wentworth stood by the old man's chair. "No, sir. I don't think you failed him. In fact, I know you didn't fail him."

The tentacle-like fingers clutched Lyon's hand. "Thank you," the old man said, and his eyes were bright.

"JESUS, LYON," Beatrice shouted. "Call your Congressman."

"Come on, Bea. You're my State Senator."

"Damn it all, hon, the welfare mothers are going to streak the Governor's mansion today unless I get some action out of committee."

Lyon glanced down the hallway of the state capitol's crowded second floor. The House and Senate were due to go into session within minutes, and the hall was crowded with legislators, lobbyists, and assorted constituents. Down the hall and marble staircase he saw the stalwart women of the Antivivisectionist League marching through the crowd, and he knew they'd make for Bea as soon as they saw her. Since none of the legislators except the majority leader had offices, a certain pecking order existed concerning the marble pillars in the hallway. Beatrice, by seniority and outspoken views, had the third pillar from the stairs, only three removed from the state chairman. So it was here that Bea met with her constituents, fellow legislators and occasionally her husband.

The Antivivisectionist group was almost at the head of the stairs, and approaching from the other direction was Kimberly leading a covey of welfare mothers.

Lyon grasped Bea's arm and led her firmly into the Senate majority leader's office.

"If I've told you once, I've told you for three terms, Lyon. There's no place to screw in the Capitol. You just have to wait until I get home."

The young secretary looked up from her desk with bewilderment and quickly fled the office.

"Knock it off, Bea. And get your hearing aid fixed."

She put her arms around his neck. "There is a large broom closet in the . . ."

"Two phone calls, Bea."

"Two quick ones."

"Please. One to Washington, the Senator's office; one to the State Banking Commission. An imperative rush. Have them call me at home this afternoon."

"What do you need to know?"

He handed her the slip of paper as she resolutely picked up the telephone.

"Sarge's" Bar and Grill was never the local "in" spot. It housed a neighborhood bar in a house set back from a secondary highway with living quarters for the owner upstairs. The bar's interior was functional in its utilitarianism—a long bar with ten stools, wooden floors, and half a dozen booths. The interior decorations, for the most part, were beer company photographs of young women in bathing suits, holding beer cans, next to canoes. On the bar were large jars filled with pickled eggs, pigs' feet and other unappetizing assortments which no one ever seemed to eat or buy.

The owner, Sarge Renfroe, was a heavy-set, bulbous-nosed Army veteran of twenty years who'd come to Murphysville some years before to visit

Rocco Herbert, his old company commander. He had stayed on, seeming to feel that there were distinct advantages in opening a bar in a town where his old commanding officer was the chief of police. He'd been right. On countless nights Rocco had come by at closing time and taken the half-unconscious owner upstairs to his bedroom after he'd sampled too much of his own products.

Lyon had been trying to reach Rocco all afternoon, and the only response from his office had been that he was out on a very important investigation. Requests to raise him by radio had failed, and finally, after leaving word with Kim where he'd be, Lyon had driven too fast down to "Sarge's Place."

Rocco was in the far booth, a small glass of beer cuddled in his hands as he stared out the window.

The Sarge waved at Lyon with a dirty bar rag. "I've heard of hidden speed traps," Lyon said, "but this is ridiculous."

"I've got a direct view of a stop street," Rocco replied. "Had some of my best days just sitting here."

A glass of sherry miraculously appeared in front of Lyon as he settled opposite Rocco in the booth. "Our time's almost up," Rocco continued with a glance at the large clock over the bar.

"Rocco, you know damn well that the Sarge's clock is the only bar clock in the state of Connecticut that runs forty minutes fast . . . you set it that way yourself."

"It takes the slob that long to close out; otherwise I'd be busting him every other night for violation of closing hours."

"I think I may have it," Lyon said.

"Thinking isn't good enough, Lyon. I can't sit on this thing any longer. In a few more minutes I have to see the first selectman, and we've got to call in the state."

"All right, do that. But before you do, call a press conference and release the names of the victims."

"Sure. We can make up what we want, any good titles . . . like your books. We can call them the Ghouls in the Graves, the Corpse in the Cove. Do you know what I've calculated? I'll tell you what I've calculated. The number of traffic tickets and domestic squabbles I'm going to handle between now and retirement. It's up in four figures. That's a lot of people to yell at."

"You are depressed."

"Jesus, Lyon. I'm sorry. I hate self-pity. It's just that we seemed so close."

The Sarge stood next to the booth with a phone in his hand. "For you, Lyon." He handed Lyon the receiver. "Some dame claims she's from a U. S. Senator's office."

Lyon took the phone. "Yes . . ."

Immediately after the call from Washington, he received the second call from the State Banking Commission. He gestured to Rocco and was handed a small pocket notebook. At the completion of the call he hung up the phone and walked slowly back to the booth.

"We've got it," he said to the expectant chief.

"How so?"

"Social security records indicate that a Meyer Meyerson was definitely employed by the Houston Company in 1942 and 1943. Company payments were made on his behalf. No further payments have ever been credited to his account."

"That's almost enough."

"The Meyersons left a three-thousand-dollar savings account in the Hartford Savings Bank. The money was never claimed and eventually was turned over to the state."

Lyon proceeded to tell Rocco about the rabbi and the disappearance of his most devout temple member, about the address which had been a trailer park, and the school records never forwarded.

"It's circumstantial, but almost positive," Rocco said, trying to control his rising excitement.

"Plus other things," Lyon continued. "No more social security payments; immigration records, police and FBI records are all negative after 1943. In 1943 the Meyerson family disappeared."

"Someone called the school and said they'd moved to California."

"And also told other people."

"Whoever did that wasn't a madman."

"No. A very calculated move to hide their disappearance. And it worked. It worked for thirty years."

"Whoever pulled it off must have known the family, known where the child went to school, where the man worked, what temple, that they didn't have relatives to ask questions."

"And now," Lyon said. "I think it's about time for you to call in the newspapers and give them what we have."

"And the State Police?"

"Let them come in too. Tell them even though the bodies were found in Murphysville, they might have been killed in Hartford or places in between."

"And we drop out."

"No," Lyon said. "We don't drop out at all. We continue."

"YOU'VE GOT TO STOP IT!" Bea stood in the center of the small study, her eyes bright with conviction. "YOU'RE NOT LISTENING, LYON."

Lyon stood before two card tables placed along the bookcase wall and stared at their object-filled surfaces. The tables were strewn with photographs of the grave, his own aerial photos, copies of Rebecca's school records, copies of temple records, and a picture of the leading temple elders during the early forties. There was a picture of a temple picnic which showed the serious Meyerson standing to the far right of the somber group. A stove ring rested in the center of the table, its measurements as close as Lyon could recall to those of the small stove in the submerged trailer.

"It's not healthy," Bea continued. "You've become obsessed with this thing." She strode to the desk and lifted the partially completed manuscript of his book. "How long since you've written a word on Cat? Not a line since this business started."

"Did you say something, hon?" Lyon asked.

Bea dropped the manuscript and put her arms around his neck. "I'm wondering if you're becoming more flakey than you used to be."

He kissed her. "The same degree of flakiness—

promise." He kissed her again. "Hey, we have to watch Rocco on the six o'clock news. He's making the announcement about the identification."

"Then that's the end?" his wife asked.

Lyon turned toward the card table with its multiple objects, the shape and form of the long-dead man beginning to become clear. A proud but tough man, devoted to his wife and daughter, devout in his religion. A man who'd fought to save his wife and himself from the horror of Hitler's Germany, who'd forged ahead with a new life, and probably a meticulous and ethical craftsman. The small family unit, together now forever in death, became clear to Lyon. His research carefully placed each piece together, and a personality took form through his investigation of the dead man's life. A savings account, carefully added to each week, old night college records showing a man's slow but careful achievements in English and engineering . . . the concern for his daughter's welfare, and a man who held his rabbi in reverence while proportioning a part of his life to the temple.

"I know this man," Lyon said aloud.

"WHO KILLED HIM?" Bea asked.

"That's what doesn't make sense. I know this man. I know what he was and what he wasn't. There wouldn't be large amounts of money in the trailer. I can't imagine him involved in an extra-marital affair. His murder doesn't make sense."

"Yes, it does. It certainly does. In a senseless and insane way. You're refusing to draw the inescapable conclusion."

"Which is?"

"A senseless thing without purpose done by a madman who's probably long dead or senile in some institution. Isn't that the logical answer?"

"It could be, if it weren't for the great care and planning to hide their bodies and identities." Lyon remembered the first senseless mass murder he had read about as a child. He had followed the case of the poison murders in the newspapers. They had all taken place in orange drink–hot dog shops; the murderer would drop poison into the soft drink of whoever happened to be standing next to him. He'd leave and stand a short distance away to view the stricken flailings of his victim. For weeks afterwards Lyon wouldn't sit at a drug store counter. Senseless and haphazard, and the records were filled with countless examples of victims whose only sin had been in being in the wrong place at the wrong time.

"You and Rocco have done a remarkable thing," Bea continued. "The bodies will be interred properly, with proper headstones. No one can expect more."

"It's almost time for the local news on television," Lyon said, taking her arm and leading her through the house to where the television sat sullenly blank.

As Bea adjusted the set, Lyon stared through the large window at the river below the hill. A brisk wind rippled its surface, and he could see a small girl in a white dress walking across the wavelets carrying a Sonja Henie doll. The sun was dimming behind the hills, and her face was diffused in the half-light.

"If there isn't action by the Governor, I will take this to the floor of the Senate!"

"You don't have to proselytize me, Bea," he said, and then saw his wife simultaneously leaning back on the sofa and also on the television screen being interviewed by a young announcer in the hall of the Capitol. "I didn't know you were going to be on. We could have come in earlier."

Bea smiled at him from the sofa as her image disappeared from the screen, to be replaced by an uncomfortable Rocco Herbert. In stilted tones Rocco outlined the facts, the finding of the bodies, the investigation and the final identity of the victims. He indicated Lyon's participation as that of a concerned citizen, without name. Rocco concluded the short interview with a request that anyone knowing the family should contact him or the State Police at once.

Lyon turned off the set as a pretty blond weathergirl stared somewhat blankly at a meteorological map. Fifteen minutes later they were halfway through the first cocktail when the phone rang. They looked at each other from their respective ends of the couch.

"It's probably Rocco calling to find out if he did well," Lyon said.

"No. The welfare mothers calling to say my statement was too wishy-washy."

They smiled at each other over the rims of their glasses, but the spell was impossible to maintain with the incessant ringing of the phone. "You know," Lyon said, "I understand that the phone company can put a switch on the box so that you can't hear it ring."

"If you take it off the hook it makes all sorts of weird noises," Bea said.

Lyon reluctantly lifted the receiver. "Yes?"

"Mr. Wentworth?"

"Yes."

"Mr. Houston would like to speak with you. One moment, please."

Lyon held the lifeless phone in his hand and looked at Bea. "Who the hell is Houston?"

"Houston? Asa Houston," Bea said. "Houston Company and half the state of Connecticut."

Lyon shrugged as a sonorous voice greeted him. "Lyon Wentworth," the voice said and continued without pause, "I've just spoken with Chief Herbert and he tells me that you were primarily responsible for identifying those people recently found in the grave."

"We worked together," Lyon said.

"I also understand that the man worked for my company," Houston said. "And if you know anything about my reputation, you know that I have extreme concern over the welfare of my employees . . . living or dead. I would like to talk to you, say cocktails and dinner tomorrow at six. My home, if that's convenient?"

"Yes, that would be fine." Lyon felt that the invitation was offered more as an edict.

"Excellent. We'll look forward to seeing you." The phone was silent and Lyon slowly hung up.

"He wants me for dinner tomorrow," Lyon said. "Forgot to ask him where he lives."

"I know where it is," Bea said. "You can hardly miss it."

Prospect Street in the capital city is a wide tree-lined avenue divided in the center by a shrub- and grass-covered mall. In bygone years the large homes and circular drives with wrought iron fences had been the abode of insurance company presidents and factory owners. In recent years many of the wealthy had made the exodus to exurbia, selling to church and school groups. Only the very wealthy, able to afford the retinue of required servants, remained in the large homes. Houston's home was directly across from the Governor's mansion. Several years ago when there was talk of running Asa Houston for Governor, political columnists had jibed that for him a move to the Governor's mansion would be a comedown.

Lyon turned in the driveway, barely missing a large cement fence post, and as the rear wheels of the small car slithered on the gravel, he braked to a halt behind a large limousine.

"Asa Houston," Bea intoned in a monotone as if reading from the daily register at the legislature, "Owner of Houston Company and Houston Transportation, and a major stockholder in the *Hartford News*, Channel 5, and other interests. A Horatio Alger story. Born of poor but honest parents, by dint of hard work and a ruthless manner he rose to the top of the business community."

"I take it he's not a campaign contributor of yours?" Lyon said.

"Very funny," Bea said as they left the car. "As I recall the invitation, he asked you for dinner. When he sees me he's going to have apoplexy."

They could hear the door chime in the house interior, and before the resonance was complete the door was opened by a well-tailored butler. "Mr. and Mrs. Wentworth," Lyon said, and they were ushered toward the living room.

The large double doors of the living room were open, and as they poised in the frame, Lyon could see several couples standing in the center of the room near the fireplace, holding cocktail glasses and engaged in animated conversation. He immediately recognized a retired general, the president of one of the city's largest insurance companies, the Lieutenant-Governor, and the director of the ballet school, who was currently in heated debate with a stately woman twice his size.

She seemed to appear instantly before them. She smiled, but behind the welcome Lyon sensed the subtle sexuality of a Garbo or Bergman, a look combined with a certain slant of cheekbone and eye configuration that hinted of a hidden understanding. She appeared to be in her late thirties, and yet he knew that in reality she was fifty. Her figure was mature, yet exquisite in its dimensions, the conservative black cocktail dress with its single strand of pearls accenting in good taste the very essence of the woman before them. One of the few women you find who are cool, beautiful, and ageless, while exuding sexuality and intelligence. He felt Bea's arm slightly tense on his as the woman held out her hand.

"You're the Wentworths. I'm so glad you could come. I'm Helen Houston. May I call you Bea, Mrs. Wentworth?"

"Of course," Bea said and Lyon could detect a slight hint of surprise in her voice.

"I can't tell you how much I've admired your work in the Senate. I'm really quite a fan of yours." She dropped her voice in a tone of mock conspiracy. "Sometimes I watch your press conferences in the kitchen. There are certain elements here that disagree with many of your stands."

Bea laughed, and Lyon felt her arm unflex as she shook the other woman's hand.

"Come on, you two," Helen said. "My husband can't wait to meet you." They joined the group in the center of the room, and drinks of their request were delivered while introductions were made. Even among this assemblage, Asa Houston dominated the room. As tall as Lyon, but with broader shoulders, he had a shock of pure white hair and features that had aged with deep character lines. As so many extremely successful men do, he radiated assurance.

"Wentworth," Houston said with extended hand. "Glad you could make it. You look very familiar. We've met?"

"No, I don't think so," Lyon replied.

"You have a short memory, darling," Helen Houston said, taking her husband's arm. "A few weeks ago he was on the front cover of *Connecticut Magazine* . . . in his balloon and holding a bottle of champagne."

"Every Sunday," Bea said tiredly.

"Why the champagne?" Helen asked.

"An old ballooning custom," Lyon replied. "Since we never know quite where we're going to come down, it's to be opened and given to irate farmers . . . or golfers."

"Since I manufacture airplane engines, let's hope it doesn't catch on," Asa Houston said with a laugh as they went in to dinner.

It was over dessert and coffee that Asa Houston turned to Lyon and asked him about the identification of the bodies. The rest of the diners were engrossed in their respective conversations. Bea at the far end of the table was in an animated dialogue with the Lieutenant-Governor, and the general was patiently explaining to the vibrant Mrs. Houston the make-up of an infantry division.

"How did you get involved in that business?" Houston asked. "I'd say it's a rather unusual avocation for a children's writer."

"Chief Herbert and I are old friends. I suppose you could say that I went out initially as an observer, and then it became a problem in logic."

"Fascinating. Tell me, step by step, exactly how you went about it."

Under Asa Houston's probing, Lyon recounted the investigation. When he had finished, he found that he and Houston were alone in the library, Lyon holding a snifter of very good brandy, Houston coffee.

"As I was saying," Houston said, "it seems to me that you had a good deal of luck. If your initial supposition had been incorrect, or if you hadn't had such a far-fetched theory, it would have been an impossible job."

"You're probably right, but like a great many other things, the element of luck or fate can't be discounted."

Asa Houston leaned back in his chair and crossed his arms behind his neck. "Meyerson," he said aloud. "I can't recall the man. My interest in this whole matter, Lyon, is the fact that the man did work for me, did live right next door to the plant. I'd like to see justice done. If I could only recall the man . . . but recalling a great many things during that period of my life is difficult." He tapped his coffee cup. "I didn't drink coffee in those days. In fact I made a valiant effort to drink the distilleries dry, but they won and I quit. And another thing, when the war started I had a small machine shop with hardly a dozen employees, and I ran a lathe right alongside them. By the time the war ended I had a factory employing over twelve hundred. Those days were a whirlwind. A lot of the details blur, and we had hundreds of employees in and out. Some of them worked a couple of months and moved on, others were hired and tried to train but couldn't . . . a blur, a real blur."

"Well, no one expects you to recall your employees of thirty years ago," Lyon said.

"Damn it all! I have an obligation to that poor bastard and his family. Just like I have an obligation to my present workers. Are you still going to continue with it?"

"Yes, I'm afraid I'm caught up in it."

"Well, there is one thing I can do. I'll call my personnel manager first thing in the morning. I personally guarantee the cooperation of my whole staff."

"I'd be very appreciative."

"Oh, by the way, are there any leads . . . anything further to go on?"

"Yes, a couple of items that I haven't released to anyone. Mostly speculation at this point, so I'd just as soon not go into them."

Asa Houston took Lyon's arm as they walked back to the living room. "It seems to me," Houston said, "that to this point you've done pretty damn well with your speculation."

"Perhaps," Lyon replied. "Perhaps."

Five

The Fox in the Factory.

As he looked through the room-length windows overlooking the factory complex, the idea came full-born to Lyon. Froelich Fox danced along the distant water tank and then appeared on the roof of the foundry, only to scamper along the conduit pipes toward building number three. Undoubtedly he'd have a comfortable lair hidden deep in the recesses of the warehouse. The idea was well-shaped, and Lyon felt the excitement that preceded the actual writing of the book.

He turned from the window and sat down at the large conference table. In front of each place was a legal pad and well-sharpened pencils. He began to make notes at a furious pace.

"You've got something," Rocco said from the other end of the large table.

"Yes, yes," Lyon muttered without looking up.

"I knew you would, I knew it." Rocco came around the table and stood behind Lyon to peer over his shoulder at the pad. "Jesus H. Christ," the large man said. "The Fox in the Factory."

"Yes," Lyon muttered again and turned to a fresh sheet of paper.

"Christ, man, we're looking for a murderer."

Lyon looked up. "What?"

"Oh, man." Rocco slapped the leather-backed chair

102

with both hands. A secretary appeared and began to serve coffee from a silver setting and bone china cups.

"Mr. Thompson will be with you shortly," she said and quietly disappeared.

The board of directors' conference room was on the third floor of the administration building of the Houston Company. Along one long wall, framed architect's renderings of the factory were tastefully hung. On two other walls, several of the company's products were displayed: airplane engines, circuit wire, and calibrated machine tools. The remaining wall opened to floor-length windows that overlooked the panorama of buildings comprising the factory.

Lyon folded his notes carefully and stuffed them in a rear pocket. He turned toward the windows where Rocco stood. "Big mother, isn't it?" the Chief said.

"Impressive," Lyon replied. "There's a strange beauty about a factory, the lines of the buildings, the latent power. Used to be an artist who painted water towers, dynamos, all that sort of thing—can't remember his name, but it'll come to me."

"You know, Lyon, I could be doing something useful, like checking the high school washrooms for pot."

"We have the same problem here," the voice behind them said. They turned to be introduced to Willis Thompson, director of personnel and employee relations. "Yesterday we found a young employee at a punch press stoned out of his mind. 'Chunch, chunk, what bunk' was all he kept saying."

"What did you do with him?" Rocco asked in a professional manner.

"Referred him to our employee rehabilitation unit.

103

We have a full time psychologist and family counselor on the staff," Thompson said.

Lyon judged Willis Thompson to be in his early thirties, slightly myopic, and if school ties were in vogue, his would be Harvard Business School, MBA, 1968. He placed several neat folders on the conference table, and as he talked, he proceeded to align them obsessively.

"I received a personal call from Mr. Houston. He asked that we all give you our fullest cooperation."

"Thank you," Lyon replied. "It's greatly appreciated."

"As background," Thompson continued, "I've brought some pictures and other information of historical interest. This one shows the factory in 1943." He extracted a glossy print from one of the folders and handed it across the table.

"It's sure changed," Rocco said.

The 1943 picture showed the Houston Company as a hodge-podge of quonset huts, unpainted structures, and a muddy parking lot, the total grouping one-fifth the size of the complex presently visible outside the conference room windows.

"We've grown and improved quite a bit over the years," Thompson said. "In 1943 we had a period of rapid expansion. That point in time when a small plant began to grow into a major industrial factory. You will notice the temporary nature of many of the buildings. Since then, as you can see, we have land-scaped the area and provided picnic benches, a recreation area, cafeterias, and of course full medical and dental care. I might say, we probably have the most extensive employee benefit package in the state."

"Very impressive," Lyon said.

Thompson held the photograph by its edge and carefully replaced it in the folder. "Unfortunately our records for that period are not very complete. The personnel records were destroyed. Now, of course, everything is microfilmed for permanent and perpetual storage."

"You must have some employees who were around during that period," Rocco said.

"Thirty years is a long time ago, and you have to keep in mind that then we were a struggling company. Many of the workers who came here were temporary wartime workers. Many were older men who couldn't serve in the Armed Forces, that sort of thing."

"There must be some," Rocco said.

"Well, yes, of course. Some retired and a few still here. Exactly what do you want?"

"We'd like to talk to an employee who worked here in 1943."

"Mr. Houston personally asked that we give you our complete cooperation." He opened another folder and examined it carefully a moment. "Perhaps you'd like to start with Mr. Graves. He's our senior vice-president in charge of production. He started here in 1942 as an apprentice machinist. A real success story."

"That would be fine," Lyon said. "Let's start with Mr. Graves."

"Hell, yes! I remember those years. We worked in those days, we really worked—no molly-coddling union to make rules for us. Let me tell you, one day in forty-three I worked around the clock. That's right, around the clock, twenty-four hours. No office work, either; I was on a machine in those days, a lathe man."

Jim Graves sat at the opposite end of the conference table, but his robust voice filled the room. As he talked, his expensive suit coat opened to reveal that he wore suspenders, and the aura of the factory floor still seemed to surround him.

"I started here when I was nineteen. Didn't know a lathe from a Bullard in those days. Worked right alongside Asa Houston himself in the beginning; then later on Asa had to travel down to Washington to see about the government contracts. But not in the beginning; he worked and set up just like anyone else. That's where I learned to work, and I mean really work. Not like things are now."

Lyon took the picture from his pocket. It was a blow-up of the temple picnic, with the serious Meyerson to the far right. He handed the picture to Thompson, who walked around the table to hand it to Graves. "Do you recognize any of the men in this photograph?" Lyon asked.

Graves examined the photograph, took glasses from his coat pocket, donned them and looked again at the picture. "Can't say that I do. Sure don't know this guy in the center with the beard. Nobody wore beards in those days; everyone was clean-shaven. Now, we have to put hair nets on some of the guys. Can you imagine—hair nets so they don't get caught in the machinery."

"Anyone in that photograph look familiar?" Rocco asked.

"I wouldn't recognize a picture of myself thirty

years old. Besides, all these guys look like foreigners, and look at the funny little caps."

"Yarmulkes," Lyon said.

"Oh, Jewish," Graves said. "I worked alongside a German Jew when I first started here. Serious little guy, used to practice his English while he worked. Always had a book on the bench right next to him, and all day long he'd say words over and over again. Good toolman too. Meyerson was probably one of the best I ever saw, a real stickler on the job."

"Meyerson?"

"I think so. Yes, Meyerson." Graves picked up the photograph again and examined it closely. "The one on the end, the serious little guy. That could be Meyerson."

"What happened to him?"

"Meyerson? Best thing that ever happened to me was when he left. He'd have the job I have now, no question about it, but then he moved to California. When he left, they made me foreman."

"Foreman?"

"Sure. Meyerson became foreman when he got his English down pat. A Goddamn good man."

"How do you know he went to California?" Lyon asked.

"That was thirty years ago . . . I don't know. Someone must have told me. I remember his leaving pretty clearly because of the fight."

"What fight?" Rocco asked.

"Meyerson and Bull Martin. They had it out right on the floor. Meyerson was a little guy, but spunky . . . and Bull . . . well, you don't call a man Bull if he's a ninety-pound weakling. I finally had to help stop it when Bull had him on the floor and was kicking him in the head."

"What were they fighting about?"

"I don't know. Probably something about production; Bull was a foreman too, but fights happened a lot in those days. Everyone was on edge, the long hours, no sleep . . ."

"Was Meyerson hurt?"

"Beat up. Nothing serious. As I remember, he finished the shift, and then the next day he moved away."

"What happened to Bull?"

Graves leaned back in the chair thoughtfully. "You know, I don't know. Seems to me he left the plant a little after that. I don't know what ever happened to him. I remember him though, mean as a snake."

"His first name?"

"Just Bull. At least that's what everyone always called him. Funny, if it hadn't been for those two fighting and then leaving, I'd probably still be on the floor myself. Funny."

"Yes," Lyon said. "Funny."

Lyon Wentworth's feet dangled over the edge of the hayloft; a piece of straw dangled from his lips, and a sailor's needle and heavy thread were clenched in one hand as he tried to thread the eye. The hot air balloon envelope was stretched in the interior of the barn, and after a careful examination he had discovered a small rent in the material and was now attempting to sew it.

Through the open loft door he could see, across the yard, the women approaching the barn. Martha Herbert's small but determined steps put her in the apex of the group, with Bea and Kimberly only a few feet behind. They blinked as they entered the barn and peered through its dim interior.

"ALL RIGHT, WENTWORTH. WHERE THE HELL ARE YOU?" Bea's voice filled the building.

"Gone fishing," he replied. As the women looked up at him he waved and dropped his thread spool. "Damn!" Lyon stood and turned to go down the loft ladder. "What can I do for you ladies?"

"TIME FOR A CONFERENCE," Bea said.

"Turn up your gizmo, darling," he replied.

"You're ruining my husband's career," Martha said.

"You've had it, man," Kim added with glee.

"If someone will thread a needle for me, we can all sit on the veranda with lemonade and listen to the happy darkies chant in the fields," Lyon said and gave Kim a pat.

"Make your own fucking lemonade," Kim replied.

On the veranda the three women talked in low voices, a chore for Bea, while Lyon made lemonade in the kitchen. Placing the iced pitcher and glasses on a tray, he kicked open the door and served the determined group. Sitting on the porch railing, he smiled at them. "Well?"

"We want action," Bea said. "How about something like the Tick in the Typewriter, the Bat and the Book, the Raven and the Royalties, the Moose and the Money?"

"You've sent Rocco down to Washington, and you know the town won't reimburse him for that," Martha Herbert said.

"And you know how them Washington chicks are,"

Kim said with a laugh as Martha stared daggers at her.

"Someone else could have gone to Washington," Martha said.

"It's a job for the State Police. They're equipped, they have the money, and after all, Lyon," Bea said, "it is their case now."

Kim laughed again. "The chicks down there got a new thing, called getting pinged by a pig."

Martha glared at the black girl again. "Please stop it."

"All right, all right," Lyon said. "To tell the truth, the money aspect never occurred to me. The research Rocco's doing will only take a day or two. He should be home tomorrow in time for dinner."

"Why, Lyon?" Bea said tiredly. "The police are hardly paying you a retainer for your efforts. You haven't done a thing on Cat since this whole thing started."

He explained to them about the meeting at the Houston factory. The fight between the murdered man and a man called Bull Martin. "And so," Lyon said, "now, we find a man named Martin."

"That's a very common name, and Bull is hardly a given name," Kim said.

"I know," Lyon replied. "But how many Martins worked for Houston in 1943, and where are they now?"

"This is all beginning to sound familiar," Bea said. "We've been through this one before."

"With results," he retorted.

Bea shrugged. "Isn't it time you two stopped?"

"The last I heard, Rocco was a police officer," Lyon said.

"Parking tickets, accidents, drunks and domestic squabbles," Martha said. "How many times have I heard that?"

"We need a few more days. Let's see what we can turn up about Bull Martin, find out where he is, or even if he's still alive."

"To the end of the week," Bea said. "And then I want to see only elbows and hear typewriter keys."

"Yes, dear," Lyon said. "Elbows and keys."

It took Rocco Herbert a day longer in Washington than they had expected. When he returned and came to Nutmeg Hill, the lines under his eyes, Lyon felt, were not so much from his District of Columbia research as from his wife's monologues.

In the study Rocco held the folder tightly across his knees. "Well, what do you have?" Lyon asked.

"All there is. Six Martins at Houston's during 1943. Three deceased, two I've located, one no record."

"Shall we go, Chief?" Lyon said.

"I'll drive," the large man replied.

The two Martins Rocco had tracked down lived in the metropolitan area, and within four hours they'd talked to both, discovered that one had left the plant months prior to the fight with Meyerson, and the second had been a maintenance man whose physical size and club foot ruled him out as the potential "Bull" Martin.

Back in the study during late afternoon Lyon sipped sherry while Rocco took his vodka neat—a preference he claimed to prefer, but which, Lyon felt, was to rule out possible discovery by his wife of any daytime imbibing.

"A dead end," Rocco said. "Thad Martin left the plant sometime in 1943. No further FICA payment to the federal government, no death certificate in this state . . . a blank . . ."

"He could have gone into the service."

"And been killed."

"Either he's our Martin or one of the deceased ones was."

"Could we have overlooked some point, something we haven't followed?" Rocco asked.

"There's got to be something . . . somewhere."

They sipped their drinks and watched the waning sun through the window. Lyon closed his eyes. He could see his own vague shape years ago standing before a map board in headquarters. Piled on a table in front of him were combat patrol reports, aerial photographs, company commander reports. The possibilities were diverse, the information scanty as he attempted to piece together a picture of intentions. In combat the intention of the enemy was obvious . . . to annihilate you . . . at least that had been the intention in the old wars. A missing man. A man who left a factory thirty years ago and to all intents and purposes ceased to exist.

In today's society or in the society of the forties, a man could not disappear. Somewhere there was a tracking, a sign, a print of his being and whereabouts. There was always a record somewhere.

Lyon looked at Rocco. "Suppose T. Martin were self-employed."

Rocco smiled. "Income tax, franchise tax, license fees, state registrations . . . worth a try."

"I believe it is," Lyon said and refilled their glasses.

The "Bull Pen" was located off Highway 66 on the road to the shore. They'd located their Thad Martin in the records of the liquor control commission and discovered that he was permittee for a restaurant and cocktail lounge aptly called the "Bull Pen," a name which gave them both a great deal of satisfaction.

On the three-quarters-of-an-hour ride to the restaurant, Lyon was regaled with the attributes and advantages of the town clerk's job. The orderliness of the deed and mortgage books, the possibility of running a few real estate titles for local lawyers . . . a sinecure greatly to be desired, at least according to Rocco Herbert.

They pulled into the parking lot of the "Bull Pen." It was set a hundred feet back from the highway, a large one-story building with brick veneer front and a large neon sign. A placard near the doorway announced rock bands on Fridays and exotic dancers on Saturdays. Four cars were neatly aligned along the side of the building, one a large Cadillac with a marker containing only the initials TM.

"I don't need to check motor vehicles to find out who that is," Rocco said.

The main door to the lounge was locked, and they entered through a side door with the small "men's bar" sign; along the bar three locals were sipping beer and joking with the young barmaid.

"Where's Bull?" Rocco asked.

"In the back auditioning," she replied without turning her head.

"Thanks," Lyon replied, and they walked the length of the bar toward the double doors to the rear.

"Hey, wait a minute," the barmaid yelled after them. "Hold your horses. Bull don't want no one in there when he's auditioning, otherwise we'd have half the yokels wantin' a free peek."

Rocco Herbert never broke stride, and without replying he pushed the doors open as they entered the large rear area. Inside the wide room chairs were piled on tables and the floor was freshly waxed. A ringside table was cleared and they could see the back of a large man straddling a chair near the dance floor. A lone spotlight illuminated the center of the small stage where a dancer undulated. She was down to a G-string, bent backward, her hips thrust forward, her head touching the floor. As the music over the public address system increased in tempo she straightened and went into a bump and grind routine.

She moved offstage to the center of the small dance floor near the ringside table and stood with arms stretched overhead, breasts jutting forward. She bent slowly backward again, her fingers touching the floor, hips forward toward the sitting man, and began to undulate. Quickly she stood erect and threw the G-string aside, now completely nude. She panced forward toward the sitting man, her stomach muscles rippling as she ran her hands over her breasts, the nipples erect, and then her hands went down her body to the shaved triangle between her legs. Placing one hand between her legs she squeezed and rotated slowly

114

from side to side, chirping, while the other hand reached toward the man.

The man grasped her bare shoulders and pushed her downward until she was on her knees before him. She bent forward, and from the rear of the room Lyon and Rocco could see the backward and forward movement of her head as she knelt before the sitting man.

"I like to see you flash it, baby," the man at the table said.

The dancer stopped and brushed her long hair back. "I don't mind stripping all the way for you, Bull, but if I flash it for the locals, I get busted."

"Nobody busts anybody around here without my say so, pussy cat. On the late show Saturday I like to give my customers a real treat, a couple of good flashes . . . if I get a real swinging group in here, then you go for broke."

"You put up bond money if anything happens?"

"You know it, pussy cat. Now, show me what you can do for the swingers."

"O.K., but I don't do nothin' with animals. You understand, I draw the line with dogs and stuff . . . I got principles."

"I know you do, pussy cat; now let's have a little more French."

"For the fuzz in the audience?"

Bull stood and turned, knocking the chair over. His pants were open, his erect penis thrusting forward. "Who let you creeps in here?"

"Knock it off, Martin." Rocco's authoritative voice was reminiscent of Korea years ago. "Send your pussy cat to the sand box."

Without turning, Bull Martin waved a hand and the

dancer quickly left while he adjusted his clothing. "You guys aren't from around here," he said.

"Sit down, Martin. Unless you want our conversation to take place at the State Police barracks."

Bull Martin contemplated them coolly for a moment and then set chairs around the table. "You fellows want a drink . . . on the house?"

"You are Thad Martin, Bull Martin?" Lyon asked.

" 'Course I am. What's the matter, I forget to pay a ticket somewhere?"

"Cut the crap, wise ass," Rocco said.

Lyon looked at the fat man sitting across the table from them, his pudgy hands enveloping the highball glass, his eyes glinting anger. Bull Martin wore slacks and a white shirt open at the neck; morning food stains dribbled across the shirt pocket.

"Would you like to ask this gentleman some questions?" Rocco said as he took a small notebook and pen from his pocket.

"Mr. Martin," Lyon started, "you were employed by the Houston Company in 1943."

"No."

"You never worked for the Houston Company?"

"Maybe I did when I was a kid. In 1943 I was in the service, as I remember it, a little place called the South Pacific."

"I submit you worked for Houston in 1943," Lyon said.

"You what? Listen, mister. I sure ought to know where in hell I worked, and sure in hell ought to remember a little something like the war in the South Pacific. What is this anyway? I don't have to answer questions for nobody."

"It would be of great help to us if you would," Lyon said.

"Help-smelp. Both you guys fuck off. Go on, get outa' here. This isn't your town, cop—you got no rights here."

Rocco looked at Bull until the other man averted his eyes. Slowly, very slowly, Rocco placed his notebook and pen along the edge of the table. His hand reached across the table and closed over Bull's fist.

"I also submit, sir," Rocco said in a low voice, "that you were an employee of Houston in 1943."

Rocco's hand tightened over Bull's fist as beads of perspiration formed on the fat man's forehead. "You guys get outa' here. You got no right . . ."

"Remember 1943," Rocco said as his hand tightened.

"Jesus, man, let go! You're crushing my fingers."

"1943," Rocco said again, his voice almost a whisper.

"Yeah, yeah, 1943 . . . I worked there. I went in service later."

"Now, you're doing just fine, Mr. Martin." As Rocco's large hand enclosing the pudgy fingers of Bull Martin tightened, the other man half rose, the chair falling over backward. "Now, let's see if you can recall Mr. Meyerson."

"Please . . . I don't remember anybody that long ago."

"Think again. You were both foremen."

"All right . . . all right, just let go."

Rocco released the other man's hand and picked up his pad and pencil. "I'm glad you recall Mr. Meyerson, Bull. Now . . . what do you remember about him?"

"So, I beat up a Hebe thirty years ago, what's that mean?"

"What was the fight about?"

"I don't remember. I had lotsa fights in those days." Rocco's hand made a tentative gesture toward Bull. "It was over his wife."

"His wife?"

"Yeah, I was jumping her. They lived in a trailer next door to the factory, and I'd go over there and jump her during my breaks. She loved it. The little Hebe found out and got ticked off. He tried to take me."

"What happened to him then?"

"I read the papers. I read where you found the body. Don't try sticking that on me. I heard he moved away somewhere, tried to get his wife's nooky away from me. Then I went into the service."

"How'd you open this place?" Lyon asked.

"I won a pot of dough on the troopship coming home. Everybody had a shit-ass fulla dough and no place to spend it. We played craps, I was big man, got off that boat with over eighteen grand."

"What else do you remember about Meyerson?"

"Not much. He and I didn't exactly socialize. Besides, he was always working or studying. So, I beat him up. What's that prove?"

"It proves that I want you in my office at nine o'clock tomorrow morning," Rocco said and handed a business card across the table. "There are a few items of evidence that I'd like to discuss with you."

"What if I'm busy?"

"Then we'll meet here or at your house, or wherever

118

you are. But that would make me angry, Mr. Martin, and I don't like to get angry."

The fat man rubbed his fingers and glared at Rocco. "All right, I'll be there."

Rocco hummed an old popular song as he inched the police cruiser up to seventy as they headed back to Murphysville.

"He's not exactly my sort of person," Lyon said.

"Did you expect to find St. Francis in the gutter? Lyon, I think we've got it. I really think we've got it. The way I see it, he went back to the trailer, perhaps was caught with the wife, the fight broke out again, and that was all she wrote."

"Now you're going to let him sweat overnight, worry about the evidence we might have."

"Exactly. Then in our little talk tomorrow I'll offer to let him cop a plea, offer him manslaughter. That's the best we can get under the circumstances anyway."

"I don't like it anymore, Rocco. This is where I climb off."

"If I can break the slob, we've got it; and it'll be due to you, Lyon. From here on out it's making the bastard sweat."

"How many fingers are you going to break?"

"I'm sorry it had to come to that."

"No wonder you want to be town clerk."

"We'll have a philosophical argument over morality after our fat friend comes across." Rocco began to hum again as the car's acceleration increased.

They had Bull Martin strapped in a dunking stool along the banks of the Farmington River. His mouth was open in a scream, but Lyon could not hear any sound.

"I've broken his fingers, let me at his toes!" Rocco cried. Eight vultures circled slowly overhead.

"Dunk him for confession," a host of hidden voices cried, and Lyon swung the stool with its strapped prisoner over and down into the water. Large air bubbles broke the surface, and as they rose into the air and burst, Bull's voice surrounded them.

"I jumped her and she loved it," Bull said.

"Confess," the voices cried. "Confess and it will be time to let you up."

"I confess that I jumped her," the voice from the bubbles whined.

"Let me at his toes," Rocco said and jumped up and down in an impatient strut.

"He'll die," Lyon heard himself cry. "He'll drown and then we'll never know."

"Swine should die," the voices said as the vultures were joined by hawks.

A bell began to ring and Lyon raised the dunking stool. The fat man sat complacently in the stool, hands untied, a cigar held in one pudgy fist, a highball in the other. "Tell her to flash it," the fat man said as the bell rang again.

"WHO IS IT?" Bea said, and Lyon wondered where she was. "Oh, my God!"

Lyon was awake. He turned in bed to see his wife sitting up, the phone held away from her stricken face like some obscene object. "My God," she said again. "Yes . . . yes . . . I'm so sorry." She slowly hung up as Lyon sat upright.

"What is it?" he asked.

"That was Martha Herbert. Rocco's in Hartford Hospital. They think he's dying."

It was 3 A.M. before Lyon got to the hospital. He turned quickly into the emergency parking lot and hurried into the waiting room where he was directed to the fifth floor. Lyon hated hospitals. The prevailing antiseptic order, the sterility of color and the usual haughty manner of hospital personnel filled him with a sense of foreboding anxiety and death. Martha Herbert sat in the small waiting room on the fifth floor near the nurses' station and elevator. Her brother, Captain Norbert of the State Police, paced nearby.

"My God, Martha! What happened—how is he?" Lyon asked.

The gaunt face looked up at him. "They say he can die, Lyon. They say he might not live the night." Her brother put his hand on her shoulder.

"He's been out of surgery over an hour; perhaps we can find out something," the State Police officer said. "You stay here, Martha." Taking Lyon's arm firmly, he led him down the hall toward Rocco's room, where they talked in hushed whispers.

"My God, won't someone tell me what happened?" Lyon asked.

"Hit and run. He stopped to aid a stalled car on Sommers Road and was walking back to the cruiser to radio for a wrecker when some jerk in a large car ran him down. He'd have bled to death in minutes if the guy he'd stopped to help hadn't managed to fumble with the cruiser's radio and get a call off."

"How bad is he?"

"He was thrown over thirty feet and has a fracture

121

with internal hemorrhaging. If he weren't such a big hunk it would have killed him."

"What are his chances?"

"Ten to one against him unless he makes it through the night. . . ."

The room door opened with a bang as it thudded against the wall. The large man stood holding the door knob for support, the hospital gown barely past his groin. Lyon and Captain Norbert turned to see Rocco Herbert supporting his weight on one leg, his bruised, bandaged face contorted in pain.

"Oh, Jesus," Lyon said.

The IV needle with a portion of tubing was still attached to his arm; a protruding nose hose dangled across his face, his features a caricature of the man Lyon had been with that afternoon.

In the hallway behind them a nurse gasped, her voice a squeak. "Chief, get back into bed . . . the doctor . . ." She fled back to the nursing station and fumbled with a telephone. They could hear her frantic voice yelling into the phone. "Fifth floor, station one . . . stat . . . stat . . ."

"They tried to kill me, Lyon." The voice was barely intelligible. He held the door with both hands in order to support his weight.

Lyon and Norbert grasped him by the arms and half-carried the large man back to bed.

"They tried to kill me," the bruised face growled. "It swerved . . . I never saw it coming. It swerved toward me at the last moment . . . intentional." They managed to wrestle him into bed as arms flailed across their shoulders. Down the hall they heard running feet. "No way . . . the bastards won't kill me

. . ." The voice broke into a gurgle as the chest heaved.

A resident and an intern followed by three nurses rushed into the room. Lyon and Captain Norbert were unceremoniously pushed aside as the doctors bent over the stricken Rocco.

"It's impossible, patently impossible," the resident said. "He should have been out for hours."

"The bastards won't get me . . ." Rocco's voice trailed off as a hypodermic injection took effect.

At ten in the morning the senior orthopedic surgeon and an internist came to the small fifth-floor waiting area. "He's going to make it," the surgeon said. "God only knows how, except that he's the toughest man I've ever seen."

Martha Herbert cried noiselessly into her hands as Captain Norbert sank into a chair. Lyon stood numbly, hearing, but still seeing the contorted face of his friend in the doorway.

On the drive home Lyon Wentworth was followed. Perhaps if he'd been trained or hadn't been so weary from the experience at the hospital he would have noticed it earlier. In fact, it wasn't until he took a turn over Piper's Brook Road, neglecting to notice the detour sign, and came to a barricade in front of the washed-out bridge that he realized that another car was on the road behind him. His little car turned easily in the cramped space, and he sped up as he headed back to the main junction.

He passed the car midway down the small country lane, and as he passed, the figure in the seat turned away.

Six

Two Shirley Temples, two little girls and a Sonja Henie sat on the flat rock having a tea party. The Shirley Temples were almost identical, although one wore a white dress with red polka dots, the other a sailor suit. Sonja Henie, her skates glinting in the sun, seemed not at all awed by the company, and sat most regally while the other little girls arranged the curve of her feet in order that the sharp little skates did not cut into the tea cake. The little girl with dark hair solemnly poured.

From a nearby rock Lyon Wentworth shook his head and the scene began to fade. The child with the dark eyes turned to him, questions in her eyes, as the illusion disappeared.

Lyon stood at the edge of the excavation. No vestige remained of the crowded scene of a week before. The woods were quiet, the country lane below empty of automobiles except for his, parked along the stone wall.

The bottom of the grave, hidden from sunlight, was dark, and he wondered what they had done with the remains of the little girl.

He had been at a loss since Rocco's accident. The State Police had picked up Bull Martin, questioned him as long as they could, and released him for lack of evidence. The exasperating point was—there really wasn't any evidence. A fist fight thirty years ago, a car parked by the washed-out bridge . . . nothing, not even of circumstantial nature. Lyon had driven back to the "Bull Pen" only to be told by the barmaid that Bull had taken off for a trip to the "dogs" in Florida.

Nothing, yet he couldn't work on the book, couldn't concentrate, and even ballooning held no appeal. He'd driven back to the "Bull Pen" a third time, only to be told again that Bull would be gone for an indefinite period.

He walked around the edge of the grave, knowing full well that between Rocco's men and the State Police, the area had been combed and searched for hundreds of yards in every direction. There had been little hope that useful evidence would be discovered, but the task had been performed diligently.

An internal dark fluttering made him uneasy. Something was wrong, a subliminal apprehension impossible to articulate. He had always believed that a problem, any problem, could be solved if enough time were spent in attempting to locate a solution. He walked slowly toward the top of the ridge, finding that a large cleft in a formation of glacial boulders made an almost natural path from the grave site.

At the top of the ridge he could turn in one direction and see his car near the stone wall, and in the other the small lake nestling in the valley. He started down the opposite side toward the lake.

A day, more likely an evening, thirty years ago. They wouldn't have been killed here. They must have been killed in the trailer park and then brought here; but done in such a manner that no sound, no hint of what transpired alerted surrounding trailers.

It was hard to imagine Bull Martin involved with

Mrs. Meyerson . . . but then perhaps it hadn't been voluntary on her part . . . more likely than not, from the little he knew of Bull. A fight, a struggle . . . a large man striking at Meyerson in a rage, and then blows over and over again raining down on the remainder of the small family. A senseless killing by a senseless man. If that were so, then future clues would be more difficult to find.

He had reached the edge of the lake. Green translucent water held no secrets anymore. Across the small lake the surface rippled slightly from a spring breeze. On the far shore a hill rose steeply toward a granite ridge similar to the one he had just walked across. The lake nestled quietly in a protected valley, the only direct access a small logging road that ran through a cleft alongside the rushing stream that ran from the lake, past the remains of the grist mill and along the hill to the side.

A school of small fish swam from the bank and eddied in a circle. Lyon smiled and knelt to reach into the water.

The second thunk quickly followed the first as the water rippled three feet to his front. The noise of the shots reverberated and echoed from the hill across the lake.

Lyon stood up angrily. The shots had come from behind him. If he hadn't bent forward at that exact moment to reach into the water, the trajectory of the bullet would have carried the shots directly into the back of his head.

Damn reckless people. He strode forward. "Hey!" he yelled. "Look out what you're doing!"

The third shot ripped through the thin fabric of his

light shirt and passed through the skin of his forearm. The velocity of impact spun him in a half circle, knocking him to the ground.

My God, they must be using an elephant gun! he thought. He held his hand over the hole in his arm. Luckily, the bullet had missed artery and bone and passed cleanly through the flesh of his forearm. His first thought was that the sniper was probably at the top of the ridge; secondly he thanked God that the bullet had missed bone. A high-powered projectile striking bone could reverberate through his body, paralyze the heart valves, and cause death.

A bullet ricocheted off the rock immediately to his front, and he belly-whopped behind the protecting granite.

His arm was bleeding profusely and he ripped the shirt sleeve open to the shoulder. The wound was clean and for the moment wasn't dangerous. Using his free hand and his teeth, he tied his handkerchief over the wound as tightly as he could. It staunched most of the bleeding, and he huddled closer to the rock.

As with most nonviolent men, disbelief filled Lyon. Initially, it hadn't occurred to him that the shots were intentional; he supposed that they had to be a stray round from a hunter, but in the spring? Or then, perhaps some kids out for some plinking—with a thirty-caliber weapon? The repeated shots, and then the wound with the final ricocheting round off the protective rock, clinched the possibility. . . .

They were trying to kill him.

Lyon glanced back at the water to estimate where the rounds had hit the water when he bent over. Turning, he saw the spot where he had stood when the bullet had hit him . . . a few feet to the side of his present position. He estimated the trajectory of the rounds as on a descending incline; the shots must have come from up the ridge. The sniper lay in a concealed position somewhere along the ridge line, in a straight line perhaps two hundred yards away.

His quick movement in bending over the water had saved him. He recalled that he'd stood on the bank in upright position for a minute or two, then with an abrupt movement bent downward. The prone assassin had a scope, had taken careful aim . . . and miraculously missed because of Lyon's bending forward.

His quick movement had been sufficient to disconcert the rifleman momentarily so that the third shot, the one that had caught him in the arm, had been a foot to the side; the difference between a flesh wound in the arm and instant death.

The only way out of the small valley was up to the logging road, past the grist mill and down to the highway . . . several hundred yards, a quarter of a mile at least . . . most of it across open space. The other alternative would be to go back over the ridge to his own car, if he could ever get that far.

Lyon tried to recall the amount of traffic on the country lane that ran past the stone wall where his car was parked. He had been at the grave site for what he calculated as half an hour, and during that period he could not recall one car passing on the road below. No help of any sort from that source. A shot fired on this side of the ridge would echo among the hills. Anyone passing would hear distant rifle fire from an unknown direction, not a particularly unusual incident, not alarming enough in itself to provoke anyone to notify the police.

They were going to kill him.

The sniper would wait patiently on the ridge, biding his time and counting on Lyon's impatience. He would assume that Lyon would stand, run, make some movement away from the protecting boulders.

If Lyon stayed in his present position, the rifleman would eventually begin to work his way down the slope. He would walk slowly, rifle at the ready, always keeping a clear field of fire between himself and Lyon's position.

He had been fired upon those few times he'd been at the front lines during the Korean War. How different. An impersonal automatic weapons burst, a stray artillery round . . . the difference between impersonal war and the hunted being stalked. The situation was quite clear. The sniper had full protection, no doubt aware that Lyon had no weapon, that the location was so remote as to virtually guarantee a time element necessary for the leisurely stalking.

It was 5 P.M. Three hours to full darkness. An impossible wait.

Lyon could imagine the sniper at the top of the ridge shifting his weight to a more comfortable position, glancing toward the tree tops to check windage, positioning the rifle and scope so as to have a clear sight picture of the protecting boulder. He would be prepared for a quick shift to the right or left, assuming that Lyon might stand quickly and run for nearby cover or back toward the road. He would consider the possibility that Lyon might crawl, hoping that a low profile would offer some protection at the sacrifice of speed.

Lyon estimated that it was twelve or fourteen feet to his right until several large pines offered any appreciable cover. In the intervening distance only two small bushes provided the smallest hindrance to a clear field of fire. To his left was a small ring of stones where some long-ago hunter had built a camp fire, and beyond that a string of pines another fifteen or twenty feet away.

How long did it take a man to run a mere twenty feet? Less than ten yards, less than a first down, the length of an ordinary room. Three seconds . . . two . . .

Probabilities and timing clicked within Lyon. Assumption, the placement of the initial two shots that hit the water over his head would mean that the sniper was using a rifle with mounted scope. Assumption, he would most probably consider that Lyon would make a break to Lyon's left, his right, which would be toward the mill and the exit road.

The panic welled up and he had an inordinate desire to urinate. He recalled an automobile accident of ten years before. The car out of control on an icy hill, the swerving and then the moment of unmistakable knowledge that heavy damage if not serious injury would be the outcome. At that time he had the same feeling: Not to me . . . this can't be happening to me.

He had survived then; he wondered if he would now.

He fought panic and tried to concentrate on the possibilities, his only chance for survival. He couldn't stay where he was. In time the sniper would move slowly down the hill, past the logging road toward the rocks where Lyon lay. Then . . . at point blank range . . . a shot . . . into the lake with his body.

A dash to other protective cover would be suicidal under the present circumstances. A good marksman could probably get off two shots, perhaps three . . . and he recalled Lee Harvey Oswald, not a particularly well-trained marksman, with a poor rifle, and the devastation he had wrought.

The only chance to reach side cover would be a dash to his right, away from the exit road and therefore the least expected. Secondly, if the sniper was in the process of working his way down the hill, a further time element, small as it was, would require the raising of the weapon and a snap shot. His use of a telescopic sight would be an aid to Lyon in this instance. An excellent device for distant and calculated aim, but a distorting influence for a man working his way down a ridge line and having to raise his weapon for a quick shot.

Did he have a telescopic sight? Probably. He'd have to make that assumption. When would he start down the hill toward Lyon? Or had he already started?

He glanced at his watch. Four minutes after five. He wouldn't be on his way down the hill yet. When would he come? Propelling himself with his elbows, he inched toward the left and with his face inches from the ground looked around the edge of the rock, and then quickly drew his head back behind cover.

The bullet furrowed a path in the dirt where his face had been moments before. That settled that. His attacker was still at the ridge line in a position of readiness. Was he an impatient man? Lyon would have to assume that he was, would have to assume that he was not a professional killer, but a man who knew a little about guns, perhaps hunted deer in season, and who was now intent on, if not obsessed with, killing Lyon Wentworth. How long would an impatient man wait? His only chance lay in making a quick dash to the side while the man was working his way down the hill, when the rifle was not at the ready and trained at the rock formation. Lyon pictured the downward slope of the hill, the ridge top, the probable spot among the boulders where the assassin waited.

He imagined himself the rifleman, the gun resting across one arm, the stock against his shoulder. He could feel the stock, the metal of the trigger guard . . . semi-automatic . . . the scope with the cross hairs centered at the rock. Lyon waited . . . Lyon waited to kill Lyon . . . he lay along the ridge top and waited for himself to stand and run for the mill . . . he waited and knew how much he wanted to kill.

Five-sixteen. Lyon on the ridge was impatient. He wanted to shoot . . . he wanted to kill and get it over with. He slowly stood, the rifle held before him. Yes. Five-eighteen. He took a tentative step forward. Another and another. To the left here, don't let that tree get between you and the rock below. Keep the rifle high, chest high, ready to swing forward instantly. Go down the hill, circle that bush. . . .

Five twenty-two. Lyon's hands perspired and his breath came in shallow gasps. He drew his legs under him until almost in fetal position and inched toward the right, away from the mill. He knew it would be impossible to stay in this position long; his legs would cramp from the awkward stance. On hands and knees with his hunched back inches below the top line of the rock, he dug his toes into the sandy dirt in sprinting position. A last look at his watch. Five twenty-five.

Lyon sprang forward, hurtling toward the protecting pines, and in the last few feet dove head first.

The shot hit the tree above him, and he rolled over into the pine brush and caught a quick glimpse of the man . . . halfway down the slope. Another shot and another. The bushes hid him from sight as the rifle rounds cut a nearby branch. The man stopped to reload.

His present cover gave him only slightly more freedom of movement, and hardly more protection than he had before. He began to inch backward, using each particle of foliage as cover, constantly going backward until his feet dangled over the edge of the lake bank.

The waiting game would be over for his attacker and he'd soon be here. He pushed himself farther backward until he felt his feet touch water. He pushed until his thighs and then his torso and head were over the bank and he lay prone in the lake water with only his head above the surface.

The lake bank rose a foot above the surface of the water with grass growing from the shore, hanging long tendrils over the edge of the bank to brush the surface of the water. He remembered the school of fish swimming out from under the bank. There would be a few inches of bank indentation. Behind the slight mat of grass growing over the bank's edge would be a small hollow, caused by the natural erosion of water as the lake level fell and rose in its yearly cycle. He turned on his back to slide his head under the bank grass. The translucent waters of the lake hid his body and he could breathe behind the thin veil of foliage.

His feet searched for and found a large boulder on the lake bottom. He wedged his toe under its cantilevered edges in order to keep his body at an angled position and his torso below the three-foot depth. He knew his face was hidden, and the beat of his heart began to slow to a more normal rhythm.

Unless his arm began to bleed more profusely he could stay in this position for an indefinite period. He would have to stay until nightfall. Now, the prime danger would be fear and panic etched to a high degree of senseless nonreasoning over the long hours' wait. He would have to think, to curb the natural propensity to jump up and run, to ignore the cramp in his left instep. Lyon felt the lake. He willed himself to be a dispassionate observer watching the ruined mill, the quiet waters, and all around this quiet spot.

Lyon Wentworth thought about frogs. He contemplated the strange wonderment of metamorphosis, the grumpy dignity of a sitting bull surveying his domain, the odd appearance of the swimming animal, eyes only protruding from the lake's surface. Lyon thought about frogs and children and the problems these small reptiles might have.

Once the sun spent itself, the surrounding hills of the small lake valley brought dusk quickly. He inched his head away from the protecting bank and slowly turned over. His feet fought for balance on the lake bottom as he slowly crawled from the water to lie on the ground.

He massaged his legs until feeling began to return

to cramped muscles. Half-standing, he crouched his way toward the tree line and lay behind a protecting pine. It was quiet except for the usual night noises. In the dim light, dark tree shadows protected him as he made his way slowly up the hill toward the ridge.

The glow of the man's cigarette revealed him at the grave site. He sat on a flat rock, rifle across his knees, and smoked impatiently. On the road below, ribbons of moonlight illuminated Lyon's waiting car. An easy shot. The assassin waited out Lyon from his vantage point. Waited for a fleeing man to run across the road toward his car.

Lyon stopped stock-still twenty feet behind the waiting man. Unheard so far, he was afraid to turn and retreat back up the hill, or even to work his way sideways in the hopes of outflanking and avoiding the waiting killer.

As Lyon ran forward the man turned, rifle in hand. Lyon threw himself forward at the hulking figure, and they both fell backward into the gaping grave.

The rifle sideways between them bit into their bodies as Lyon's fingers felt through the pudgy flesh for the fat man's throat. Their breath came in grunts as the man clawed for Lyon's face and eyes. Fingers worked their way into Lyon's mouth and pulled his lips sideways. He caught the heavy scent of nicotine as his teeth ground into the man's fingers.

Lyon's thumbs pressed against the other's windpipe until his racking gasps began to subside. His knee found the man's groin, and then he quickly let go as the other man grasped for his neck.

Lyon was out of the hole with the rifle as the fat man lay gasping. The man got to his feet with labored breath and crawled from the grave. Lyon stepped backward with leveled rifle.

"Stop! For God's sake, stop," he heard himself say in an unfamiliar voice.

The breathing of the fat man increased in intensity as he came toward Lyon.

At a range of ten feet Lyon's first two shots missed Bull Martin. The man came steadily toward him. The third shot caught him in the stomach and flung him backward into the grave with an astonished look that quickly changed to horror.

Bull lay in the grave with both hands grasping his stomach. "Help me. Oh, God . . . help me."

Lyon knelt next to the dying man. "I'll get help. You killed them. You killed them, didn't you?"

"Fuck you."

"You killed them."

"I beat him senseless . . . the bastard. I beat his damn brains out . . . he was too perfect. No tolerances, he said . . . no tol . . ."

"And the others?"

"I beat . . . beat his . . ."

The man was dead. Lyon looked at the fat body at the bottom of the grave, the hands still clutched over its abdomen. As moonlight broke through the trees Lyon saw his own body. He was covered in blood from his wound and Bull's, and his clothes were wet and streaked in mud. He swung the rifle by the barrel and let it fall through the brush. Then he began to tremble.

The nurse who came to complain about the noise was now half-squiffed and sitting on the lap of the intern who had been dispatched as the second noise-abatement emissary.

The room rocked with laughter as Rocco recounted the aftermath of his ripping off the IV and orthopedic sling. In the corner Lyon shook a container of Manhattans with one hand; the other arm was encased in a sling.

"What . . . what almost killed me," Rocco laughed, "was this intern who came in to see me the next day and told me that I wasn't allowed out of bed until they took me off the critical list."

"Where in hell did you think you were going?" the intern asked.

"I don't know," Rocco replied. "I only knew that I wasn't going to lie here and listen to everyone discuss my demise."

"You were damn lucky," Lyon said.

"YOU WERE BOTH LUCKY," Beatrice retorted.

"Have you had your hearing checked recently?" the nurse said and hiccuped.

Lyon slumped into a chair and handed the cocktail shaker to Bea. With a smile and a pat on the shoulder she proceeded to make the next batch of drinks. He looked around the room. The head of Rocco's bed raised him to a partial sitting position, while one leg extended outward in an orthopedic sling. Rocco held his glass high with a grin that swept through his bruised face. His wife, quiet for once, and even smiling, stood next to him. The intern and the nurse in the far corner were involved in an intimate, whispered conversation, while Bea poured everyone a fresh drink.

RICHARD FORREST

Lyon thought the room had an aura of a successful transatlantic balloon crossing, the discovery of the mother lode, victory over the infidels, the shooting of the Red Baron, and he wondered why he wasn't happy.

"You're looking too glum, old buddy," Rocco boomed. "None of that. You're the man of the day. I propose a toast to Lyon."

They all raised glasses, and even the intern staggered to his feet. "To Lyon Wentworth," Rocco continued. "Writer of children's fantasy, menace on highway and airway, and lousy shot."

"Hear, hear," they said and drank.

"I didn't want to kill the bastard," Lyon said.

"Why not?" Rocco replied. "I would have. Gladly."

"I should have incapacitated him by shooting him in the leg. I'm afraid I was very frightened."

"I didn't mean you were a lousy shot because of that," Rocco said. "I meant you should have hit him the first time."

"If I had any presence of mind I could have hit him over the head with the damn thing."

"No matter. You got the bastard. I'd as soon feel remorse over that pig as I would a snake. You got him and the confession; that's all that matters."

" 'I beat his damn brains out,' that's what he said."

"And that's a confession. Otherwise, why would he be after you, and why come after me? You scared the living be-Jesus out of him because you were too close."

"Now we can close the files," Bea said. "Rocco goes back to parking tickets, and Lyon to his Cat."

138

"I've got the next book," Lyon said. "It came to me recently when I had some time to wait and think. How does 'Pollywog in the Pond' strike you?"

"He's got to be kidding," the nurse said to the intern.

"I think they're all nuts," the intern replied.

An hour later Rocco had disengaged himself from the orthopedic device and was sitting in a chair opposite Lyon. The nurse and intern occupied the bed, while Bea and Martha had left to find a pizza parlor. The two men smiled at each other, the glow of partial inebriation blunting the edges of pain and briefly tinting the edge of the world with soft colors.

"Damn, I feel fine," Rocco said.

"You know, we're both lucky to be alive," Lyon replied.

"We did it, man. We found out who they were, we tracked the bastard down, and it's done."

They drank to that, and they drank to their wives and to their respective jobs, and they drank again to the solution of the crime. They were both asleep in their chairs when the wives returned with pizza.

With the aid of hospital personnel, Bea and Martha carried Rocco back to bed, ushered the intern and nurse out, and placed Lyon in a wheel chair and pushed him to the emergency exit, where Bea poured him into the car. Lyon awoke as the car pulled in the drive at Nutmeg Hill.

"I bet you think I'm squiffed," he said to his wife.

"Of course I don't, dear. I think you're smashed out of your mind."

"You're right and you're wrong."

"I don't want to hear about it."

The car stopped by the steps, and after a bit of fumbling, Lyon managed to get the door open. He staggered up the steps and threw himself in front of the door, blocking Bea's entrance.

"You can't go in until you hear me out," he said.

Bea smiled in a resigned manner and laughed. "You're going to feel terrible tomorrow."

"I feel terrible now."

"If you're going to be sick, don't do it in the rose bushes."

"I am not going to be sick in the roses . . . I am sick here," he said and pounded his chest.

"You can sleep on the couch tonight," she replied.

"I'm glad I killed him, Bea. I'm glad he died in the child's grave."

"He would have killed you without a moment's hesitation," she said in a quiet voice.

"Maybe I enjoyed killing him. Maybe there was a great satisfaction in pulling the trigger. I did that once before in the service. I was caught on the line during an attack, and I fired. I didn't see them very well, but I pulled the trigger then . . . again and again . . . and I was glad afterward."

"Glad you were alive."

"Yes, glad I'm alive and glad that he's dead."

"It's over now, that's all that counts," his wife said and stepped toward him.

"You think I'm drunk," Lyon said as he stepped off the porch and fell into the fish pool. He stood to scream at his wife, the house, the river. "You think I'm drunk, and I am. But he didn't kill them, Bea. Martin didn't kill them."

140

Seven

On the couch in his study, America's greatest creator of children's fantasies awoke with a massive headache. Wind whipped rain against the window panes, and Lyon turned over to bury his head against the cushion, only to find that any possibility of sleep was gone.

"Perfect, perfect, no tolerance . . . I beat him . . ." The words synchronized with the wind and the rain as he got up. In stocking feet he trod an unsteady way toward the kitchen. He found Kimberly tacking a massive poster of Lenin to the wall near the fireplace.

"Take that off the wall," he mumbled as he rocked past her.

"Bourgeois pig," she replied without turning.

"Your vocabulary is very limited. Do we have a Coke, a soft drink, something?"

"How about a soul drink?"

"Anything."

Kimberly pushed past him and opened the refrigerator door. She handed him a large glass filled with red liquid. Lyon drained half the glass. "This is good," Lyon said and drained the rest of the liquid. "What is it?"

"Soul drink. Tomato juice, watermelon rind, clam juice, all mixed up with four shots of vodka."

"No wonder I feel better."

"You want eggs and bacon?"

"Sadist. Is Bea up yet?"

"Long gone. It's ten o'clock."

Below the hill, wind whipped the river as trees bent under the onslaught of rain. From the depths of the house he heard the chug of the sump pump, and felt surrounded by things mechanical. "Perfect . . . perfect . . . no tolerance." What did it mean?

The ringing of the phone shattered his nerves and he jerked in surprise. One hand pressed his forehead to stop the pounding as the other picked up the receiver on the kitchen wall.

"Lyon Wentworth?" the deep voice asked.

"I think so."

"Asa Houston here. I wanted to express my profound thanks for the job you performed on that Meyerson matter. And also the relief all of us at Houston Company have over your well being. You were damn lucky to come out of that incident alive."

"I'm not so sure of that either."

"What?"

"Nothing, Mr. Houston. I'm just not too well this morning."

"Well, sorry about that. Perhaps it might help if I tell you that the Houston Foundation is sending you a check for five thousand dollars as a token of our gratitude for what you've done."

"That's not necessary."

"Nonsense. You risked your life for one of my employees. Even if the man was an employee thirty years ago, he was still under the protection of Houston Company. I suppose the confession from Martin wraps it up."

"Yes, I suppose it does. Mr. Houston, he did say something to me that I don't understand. 'Perfect

142

. . . perfect . . . no tolerance.' Do you have any idea what that might mean?"

There was a slight pause. "Perfect. No tolerance. That's an impossibility, of course; a certain degree of tolerance is a necessity for any part or tool. Complete perfection is an impossibility. It's strictly a question of what's allowable under the particular specifications."

"You think he was referring to work?"

"From what I read in the paper, he said that and went on to say he beat Meyerson to death. Isn't that correct?"

"Beat him senseless."

"Same thing. I suppose they had an argument about something on the floor . . . a piece of work, set-up of a lathe or some such thing, and that's what started the whole thing. Does it matter?"

"Matter? No I suppose not."

"Once again, I can't tell you how happy we all are that the matter is concluded so neatly. You'll receive the check in the mail."

Lyon replaced the phone slowly and thoughtfully, then picked it up again and dialed the Houston Company. The operator put him through to Jim Graves, chief of production.

"Fine job, Wentworth. What can I do for you?"

"One last point. What was the factory making in 1943?"

"1943? Let me think. Same thing we now make in Department J. Of course with the prevalence of jet engines it's only a minor part of our production these days. Back in the forties it was the largest part."

"What's that?"

"Airplane reciprocating engines and components. In

1943 we were probably still making them for the B-24 Liberator, or we might have begun prototype production for the B-29, I'm not sure. I could find out if it's important."

"No, thank you. It's not important."

"Call me anytime if I can be of help."

Lyon had another of Kimberly's soul drinks and found he felt infinitely better. In fact, he felt so much better that when Kim leaned over he was able to admire the curve of her legs and thighs, and when she stood he noticed that even in faded dungarees and loose shirt she was a very attractive girl. In passing, he wondered what would happen if he made a pass at Kim, and knew instantly she'd probably kick him. For all her leftist tendencies, in certain areas she was a remarkably prudish girl. He knew what was wrong.

"YOU ARE OUT OF YOUR LIVING MIND."

Lyon reached in his wife's ear, extracted the hearing aid, turned it on and replaced it. "What did you say, dear?"

"I said, you are out of your living mind. The thing is finished. The police are happy, the state is happy, Mr. Houston is happy, and I am happy. I am very happy over the half of the money you're going to keep."

They stood in the rococo hallway of the state capitol. "It doesn't work," he said. "It doesn't fit. I knew that drunk and I know that sober. Only now I think I know the reason."

"Why would Martin come after you if he wasn't the killer?"

"I don't know. But I do know that there are still too

144

many missing pieces, and that's why I need your help."

"What evidence do you have?"

"Nothing tangible yet. But I still can't believe that Meyerson's wife would allow herself to be . . . jumped, as he put it, by that slob."

"He could have attacked her."

"There is the possibility of rape, and Meyerson could have come home while it was going on . . . a fight . . . but then what about the little girl?"

"He obviously didn't want any witnesses. He killed the woman first, then the man, and the little girl had to go."

"I stood with Martin as he died, Beatrice. He talked about tolerances, he talked about beating Meyerson . . . no mention of the child. That's one thing that doesn't make sense."

"As you said, he was dying."

"There's more to it."

"There sure is. To begin with, you don't know anything about the character of the late Mrs. Meyerson. Who knows what her bag was; she may have dug slobs. Secondly, Bull tried to kill you and almost killed Rocco. And you expect him to develop a death-bed conscience."

"I think I know what Meyerson was like, and I can't imagine his wife being of completely different character. I think Bull and Meyerson had a fight over something that happened at the plant."

"And then he went to the trailer to finish it . . . went too far and had to kill all of them."

"Why didn't he mention the child?"

"He didn't want God to hear."

"Bea, for the last time, will you please call your friend in Washington and get the information for me?"

"You know, Lyon, every time I call the Senator I have to make a commitment of political support. So far, I'm committed for his run for re-election, for his nomination for the vice-presidency and presidency . . . what this time? God."

Bea made the call to Washington and Lyon was afraid to ask what commitment she had to make. That afternoon he waited impatiently in his study until the call came from the Senator's administrative assistant.

"The name you wanted, sir, is Jonathan Coop. He presently lives at 232 Cyprus Circle, Clearwater Beach, Florida."

"Fine. Thank you for your effort."

Lyon Wentworth called the airport and made reservations on the morning flight to Tampa, Florida.

The plane touched down in Tampa with a squeak of tires on the hot tarmac. As he deplaned, Lyon squinted at the hot, bright sun reflected off buildings and concrete. With the other passengers he hurried to the coolness of the terminal building. Inside the terminal he purchased a pair of sunglasses and a map of the area before searching for the rental car agency booth.

"Master Charge or American Express, sir?" the pert young woman smiled at him over the rental form.

"Neither. I'll pay cash."

Her face fell and after a moment brightened. "Diners Club, Air Travel or BankAmericard?"

Lyon shook his head sadly.

"Carte Blanche, Oil Company Credit Card . . .

Hilton . . ." her voice trailed off as Lyon shook his head again.

"I have money," he said softly.

"Money?"

"Cash. I could make some sort of deposit."

She shook her head in great disappointment. "Telephone credit card, another car rental firm . . ."

"I have a bank account," Lyon said hopefully.

She brightened. "On a Tampa bank?"

"Would you believe Murphysville, Connecticut?"

"Would you believe a two-hundred-dollar deposit?"

"I don't have two hundred with me."

"I don't have any cars."

Four hours later Lyon waited at the Western Union counter as the aged clerk slowly counted five hundred dollars in tens onto the grimy counter. Bea had been furious. His telephone call, her trip to the bank and then Western Union had forced her to miss a roll call vote and spoiled a perfect attendance record for the session.

In another half hour Lyon was driving toward Clearwater. Clearwater Beach, connected to the mainland by a causeway, is strung along the Gulf for five miles and barely a quarter of a mile wide at its greatest width. The street atlas showed Cyprus Circle on a man-made finger to the south of the causeway.

He pulled the car to the curb at the entrance to the street. The road curved toward the water and ended in a cul-de-sac. The finger, dredged from the bottom of the Gulf, now contained three dozen neat homes with front lawns of very green grass and patios to the rear that abutted small docks along the retaining wall at water's edge. He drove slowly to the house he wanted on the cul-de-sac, close to the end of the road. He rang the bell and waited.

A stooped woman in her late fifties, her face heavily lined from constant exposure to the sun, hesitantly opened the door. "Is Mr. Coop home?" Lyon asked.

"No, he's not. If you're selling insurance or mutual funds, we don't really need any more."

"No. I'm not a salesman. I have a matter I'd like to discuss with Mr. Coop."

"He's out on the *Lorna*. That's his boat. I expect him a little after five."

"Thank you, I'll come back after that."

"Who shall I say called?" she yelled after him as he went back to the car.

"Just a friend," Lyon said. "A friend from Connecticut."

It was almost closing time by the time Lyon arrived at the county tax assessor's office, and it took a little cajoling on his part to get the clerk to pull the card on the house on Cyprus Circle. He quickly copied the information. Coop had purchased the house six years ago; it was appraised, after adjustment for percentage of value, at $70,000. Lyon wondered what sort of boat the *Lorna* was and doubted that it was an eight-foot dory or Old Towne canoe.

On the way back to Clearwater Beach he checked into a motor hotel. In his room he showered, changed, and ordered a sandwich from room service. On the room's small balcony he sat at the table, eating slowly, letting the cool Gulf breeze wash away the frustrations of the day.

The inchoate feeling that had sent him to Florida was now stronger than ever, and he had the feeling that the solution was not too distant. He was sleepy; the bed seen through the veranda doors looked very inviting. It was almost seven, time to go.

The door to the house on Cyprus Circle opened before the bell chimes finished its sequence. The man in the entryway was of medium stature. He wore thick glasses, and his thin face was deeply tanned and windblown from hours on the water.

He spoke almost inaudibly. "Yes?"

"Mr. Coop? Jonathan Coop?"

"Yes."

"I'm Lyon Wentworth. From the Hartford area. I wonder if I might talk to you a moment?"

"If you're selling something . . ."

"No. My word on that. Not even magazine subscriptions. I need some information concerning the Houston Company, something that might have happened in 1943."

"Come in, please. That's a long time ago."

They walked through the house, and Lyon felt the furtive Mrs. Coop observing them through a slightly open kitchen door. They went out onto the patio overlooking the water. The cabin cruiser was tied to the small dock behind the house and was hardly a dory. At a glance Lyon estimated its length at something over thirty-three feet. They sat at a small glass-topped table.

"Exactly what can I do for you, Mr. . . . ?"

"Wentworth. It's my understanding that in 1943 you were employed by the Houston Company."

"No. I never worked for anyone like that. I was an employee of the U.S. Government for most of my working life. General Services Administration, Army

149

Quartermaster Corps, and later on the Air Force. I retired on full pension seven years ago."

"But you were at the Houston Company in 1943?"

Jonathan Coop walked to the edge of the patio to look over the quiet water. "Perhaps you'd like something to drink?" he said.

"No, thank you."

When he spoke again it was in a low voice caught in the past. "You know, in the beginning of the depression there wasn't any welfare or relief. No, we didn't even have that honor. Occasionally the church used to send us food, then finally there were the relief trucks delivering boxes of flour and rice. They'd pull up in front of the house and you had to go down to get your food. My father was too ashamed to go and he'd send my brother and me down to get it."

"Yes, I've heard of those things."

"All day long in a half-darkened room my father would sit behind the curtains and listen to the radio. Are you sure you won't have something to drink . . . ice tea?"

"No, really, Mr. Coop. I was wondering about your stay at the Houston Company."

"That's a long time ago; I don't think about it. You know, if you work at it long enough and hard enough, it is quite possible not to think of something." He stopped—his eyes blank, without feeling. Lyon let the moment continue. "I don't suppose you're going away?"

"Not until we've talked."

"I can't imagine why you want to know anything from me. My job was always quite dull. If you're interested in finding out things about the company, there are many people who could tell you much more than I can."

"I don't believe so."

"Why do you want to know?"

"Mr. Coop . . . recently . . . a few days ago . . . I had to kill a man, and I want to know why."

"I don't understand."

Lyon explained in detail the discovery of the bodies in the remote grave, the trace and eventual identification of the Meyerson family, the location of Bull Martin and the attempts on his and Rocco's lives. He ended simply. "So, I had to shoot him."

"That's a difficult thing to do. You don't seem to be the type of person who would find that very easy."

"I don't."

Jonathan Coop took off his glasses. Even in the dimming light his eyes squinted, and Lyon had the impression of a pet mouse given him years ago as a child. A mouse who lived in a small cage and hid in the end of a tin can to peer at the world with small and furtive eyes.

"Perhaps you'd like to go out on the *Lorna* in the morning. We could leave early, go out into the Gulf and have our conversation there."

"I'm not much of a sailor."

"I'd prefer it that way, if you can spare the time."

Lyon stood. "Yes, I have the time."

"Good. Shall we say seven? I'll have coffee made in the galley."

That night Lyon had difficulty in getting to sleep. The furtive man on the veranda, the invitation to the

151

cruise . . . perhaps he should be more wary, after the experience with Bull. But Bull was dead, and it was difficult to imagine the half-frightened Coop providing any real threat. He could only conjecture from the man's nervous reticence that he wanted to be alone with Lyon, that he didn't want to talk in front of his wife. With that hope he fell asleep.

It was almost seven-thirty before Lyon arrived at the house on Cyprus Circle. The cabin cruiser's engines were idling as it bobbed at the small dock secured by two lines. As Lyon approached the dock Jonathan Coop came out of the cabin and yelled across to him:

"Throw off the lines and jump aboard. Coffee's brewed."

A soon as Lyon stepped aboard the small stern area the boat began to move slowly down the channel. Coop, on the flying bridge, yelled down that coffee was on the stove.

Lyon's estimate of yesterday as to the boat's size was correct within a foot. The boat was thirty-four feet long, with a small stern area containing a table and two chairs and the entrance to the cabin. To the immediate right of the cabin a ladder led up to the top and two leatherette seats behind the bridge.

In the cabin the saloon was nearest the stern, then a galley with eating area, head, and to the far front the stateroom. Lyon gratefully poured coffee into a mug from the pot on the stove. He drank part and then climbed the short ladder to the bridge.

"Coffee all right?"

"Just fine. Nice boat you have here."

"Thank you. I'd just as soon live on it all the time and not have a house, but my wife likes the house." They had to shout over the roar of the diesels as Coop pushed the throttles forward and the boat leaped ahead.

After ten minutes Coop turned to him. "We're in clear water. Can you hold the wheel while I go below?"

"Sure."

"Just keep it pointed straight and you'll be all right. I'll be right back."

Lyon took the wheel as Coop disappeared down the ladder. There was a partially finished cup of coffee on the deck near the helm, and Lyon wondered why the man had gone below decks. It seemed unlikely that he would attempt to prepare breakfast while the cruiser ran at three-quarter speed. He took his hands off the wheel a moment and saw that the boat still steered relatively straight. Turning, he lay prone on the deck and pushed his head over the edge of the cabin roof. By inching forward he was able to see through the top of the cabin door.

Jonathan Coop sat on the small couch in the saloon, his sleeve rolled up and a hypodermic needle in his hand. As Lyon watched, he plunged the needle into his arm and closed his eyes.

Lyon returned to the wheel and corrected the direction of the boat to its original heading. In a few minutes Coop was back beside him. "I thought we'd go about ten miles out, anchor and have some breakfast."

"Sounds fine."

When they anchored, land was barely visible at the edge of the horizon. The boat swayed gently on its lines as Coop scrambled eggs in the galley. The breakfast was simple, but excellent. Bacon, eggs, toasted muffins with marmalade and more good coffee.

"Compliments to the chef," Lyon said. "Or maybe it's that the Gulf air gives me the appetite."

"Funny how I like to cook and do mundane things at sea, and never want to do them at home."

They finished the meal and, with coffee mugs in hand, sat in the chairs at the stern. Coop stared across the empty waters toward a distant tanker on the horizon.

"Aren't you a little old for addiction, Mr. Coop?"

"Not necessarily, Mr. Wentworth. I've been addicted for some weeks now, but quite legitimately, I assure you."

"I don't understand."

"I'm supposed to receive the injections at my doctor's office, but that would mean that I couldn't be out in the boat. I was able to obtain the drugs and needle from unorthodox sources."

"Morphine?" The other man nodded. "How much time do you have?"

"It's hard to know exactly. Weeks, perhaps months. The malignancy grows worse each day . . . I don't suppose the addiction matters, does it?"

"No. I wouldn't think so."

"That's one of the reasons why I wanted to talk out here, Mr. Wentworth. My wife doesn't know about my health problem, nor some of my activities of years ago. As far as she's concerned I made quite a killing in

154

the stock market in the early sixties. You know better, don't you, Mr. Wentworth?"

"I suspected. That's why I'm here. Your life style convinced me completely."

"It's a terrible thing to be poor, and the security of a civil service job was very appealing. Then I discovered that it's a terrible thing to live on the salary of a civil servant. Things are so relative."

"No remorse?"

"None. But of course I had nothing to do with the killing of Meyerson."

"Not directly, Mr. Coop. Was it B-29s or B-24s?"

"B-24s. It doesn't really matter, but you understand that the statute of limitations has run out on this sort of thing."

"Not on murder, Mr. Coop."

"I had nothing to do with that."

"Tell me what happened."

Lines of pain crossed the man's face and he leaned back in the chair. Perspiration beaded his forehead and he wiped it with the back of his hand. "It was a long time ago. I was the inspector assigned to the Houston Company in 1943. They had their problems; lots of factories did. The spurt of growth, lack of trained personnel, shoddy raw materials. . . . It was a constant battle to produce and keep producing within the tolerances allowed by the specifications. On one particular lot, the largest the plant had produced at that time, I ran the usual tests and discovered a metal fatigue factor in the material."

"That meant government rejection of the whole shipment."

"Yes. After a hundred hours of running time, the

material stood a substantial chance of developing metal fatigue: first hairline cracks in the block, then later possible disintegration of key parts."

"Who knew about this?"

"Meyerson. That man you killed, Bull Martin. A young man who was often assigned to work with me . . . it's been so long . . . Graves. Yes, Graves, and of course Mr. Houston."

"And you never reported it to the Army Air Corps?"

"No. Houston convinced me that it would be futile, that the B-24 was being phased out of production with the conversion to the B-29 as our heavy bomber. Rejection of the shipment, at that time, would have closed the factory."

"And money."

"Yes. Money also. I had qualms then. Later on, at other factories, I developed a remarkable skill. Often, even if the specifications were met, I'd threaten rejection or at least reinspection. Rather than hold up the shipment . . . they gave me gifts. Remarkable how much money I was able to extract from so-called honest businessmen. If I do say so, I was able to perfect the routine to a fine science."

"Meyerson knew and objected to the cover-up of the defective parts. He and Bull had the fight. . . ."

"Yes. Then they told me that Meyerson quit in disgust and moved to California."

"He didn't move, Mr. Coop. At least he didn't move far."

"That became apparent to me after you left last night. Quite apparent."

"Bull Martin must have known and been bought off too."

"Yes."

"Then that's how he bought his lounge and restaurant."

"I would think so. At least that's what I told Mr. Houston when I called him last night."

"My God! You called him."

"It isn't easy to give up old bad habits. Not that the money would do me any good, but . . ." He grimaced in pain. "A little extra for my estate might ease things for my wife. Funny, there's never enough, is there?"

Lyon looked at the man across from him whose white fingers gripped the edge of the leatherette chair. He wondered how much the man's greed caused his continuing extortions, or how much was caused by an innate enjoyment he took in seeing men like Houston assume obsequious positions in their attempts to thrust money upon him. "I guess there never is enough," Lyon replied, although his context was far different than Coop's. "What did Houston say?"

"Funny," Coop replied. "At first he said he didn't remember, and I had to remind him. Then he laughed. Told me the statute of limitations had run out, that the planes involved were scrapped long ago; that no one cared about those times anymore—after all, it was several wars ago."

"That's all?"

"Almost. I told him I didn't have long left . . . and then he . . . do you know what he told me?"

"What?"

"He told me not to loiter."

"Would you sign an affidavit for me?" Lyon asked.

Coop sat upright and looked at Lyon with glinting eyes. He smiled. "How much will you pay?"

"Nothing."

"Pity." He lay back in the chair again and closed his eyes.

Lyon was on his feet. "For God's sake! You have nothing to lose. It's possible that I can use your information to find a murderer."

"I'm sorry, Mr. Wentworth. I don't see anything in it for me."

"What about the poor bastards who flew the planes with the defective parts?"

"They're dead, aren't they?"

Coop lay back in the chair to bake in the sun as Lyon went into the saloon. He found the kit in an attaché case under the divan. He opened it to find several hypodermic needles and a dozen vials with a small piece of rubber tubing. He snapped the case shut and carried it out onto the deck. He sat on the edge of the stern, one hand dangling the case over the water.

"Mr. Coop," Lyon said. "Coop!"

The other man opened his eyes, and on seeing the case held over the side of the boat sat upright. "What are you doing with that?"

"I'm about to drop it overboard."

"You wouldn't do that."

"I think I would, Mr. Coop."

"I don't think you're a very nice man, Mr. Wentworth."

"I'm beginning to wonder about that myself. Shall we go inside and begin our statement?"

With slow movements Coop went inside and sat at the dining table. From a nearby drawer he pulled out writing paper and pen. Lyon followed him in, still holding the attaché case tightly against his chest. As he sat opposite Coop he began to wonder what kind of men they were, and what kind of man he was becoming.

Eight

Rocco Herbert was comfortably positioned in "Sarge's Place" with a clear view of his favorite stop sign. The accommodating Sarge had placed a low stool for his leg cast near the window. His free arm had easy access to a stein of beer and a walkie-talkie radio. His uniform cap was neatly aligned between beer and radio.

Lyon stood in the doorway and viewed his friend benignly. "By God. I didn't think they made Bermuda shorts that big."

Rocco looked down at his shorts and cast-clad leg. "Well, I'm only half on duty."

Carefully avoiding the raised leg cast, Lyon sat at the table, opposite Rocco. Tearing himself away from the television over the bar, Sarge poured a glass of sherry and placed it before Lyon. "Can I autograph your cast for you?" Lyon said with a smile.

"Knock it off unless you want to write your Florida adventures on there. Come on, tell. Your phone call was rather cryptic."

"I will, but first, just what in hell are you doing? Even if you spot a traffic transgressor, by the time you hobble out there he'd be in Boston."

"Modern criminal methods," Rocco replied. "Beyond the knowledge of you ordinary laymen. I have here a radio." He picked up the radio and pressed the transmission switch. "Charlie, you awake?"

"Right, Chief," the eager voice answered back over the radio.

"Charlie's in a cruiser at the back of the bar. I see 'em, he tickets 'em. We've already gotten three this morning. You would have been the fourth, Mr. Wentworth, except that I felt sorry for you."

Lyon laughed. "That's the only reason I'm friendly with you. If we had any other chief in town my license would have been suspended years ago."

"Are you going to tell me what happened, or are you waiting for my leg to heal?"

"Have you ever tried to pay a motel with a check drawn on a Murphysville bank?" Lyon asked.

"Not outside of Murphysville."

"They were very unpleasant about it, and for a while I wasn't sure they'd take my cash." Lyon took Coop's affidavit from his pocket and handed it to Rocco. Rocco read it through slowly once and then went back over it. He thought for a moment. "Jesus," he said. He drummed his fingers on the table and signaled for another glass of beer. "Now, Coop was an employee of the federal government, but working at the Houston factory. Exactly how does that work?"

"Any factory engaged in government contracts has either an official inspector assigned to the plant or one who travels to the plant on a periodic basis. The inspector in charge is responsible for seeing that the contract specifications are fulfilled, that the goods, whatever they are, are up to the standards set in the original contract."

"And if they're not, he rejects them and they start over again."

"Exactly."

"So, if Coop was bought off, he'd pass shoddy or sub-standard parts."

"Right. And as I see it, at that time the plant was expanding like crazy. Houston's credit was probably stretched as far as it would go, and the rejection of a large shipment would have pushed him into insolvency."

"It points directly at Houston himself. Who else would benefit?"

"There's no one else that I can see."

They were both startled by laughter from the doorway. Sarge grinned at Rocco. "You missed one, Captain. A son-of-a-bitchin' Mercedes Benz didn't even slow down at the stop sign."

Lyon laughed. Rocco grimaced. "He who passes stop sign once will do so again and get busted," the Chief said. As best he could, he shifted his plaster-clad foot slightly and flexed his leg. "So, we have it?"

"Could be. Coop was bought, Bull Martin knew it, and then Meyerson found out about it. Meyerson and Bull had a fight on the plant floor. Meyerson still wouldn't drop it. Martin reports the state of things to Houston. Houston, seeing his new-found gains threatened, panics . . . kills the family, dumps the trailer, and tells everyone they've left for California. Bull knows too much, but can be bought off and sent into the Army."

"Then why does Bull come after us?"

"Two possible reasons. Houston paid him, or they were both in on the murders. That way he'd be protecting himself. He knew we were getting too close."

"Then Houston's the one we want," Rocco said.

"With Bull dead, it's going to be hard to tie this to Houston."

Rocco Herbert pressed the transmission switch on the radio. "Wake up, Charlie."

"Jeez, Chief. I was only resting my eyes from the glare."

"There's no glare back there, Charlie. You're in the shade."

"Yes, sir."

Rocco and Lyon stared out the window into the late morning sun. The Sarge was nodding sleepily at the bar, while one other customer nursed a small beer and looked at himself in the bar mirror. The only sound was the faint hum of the refrigerator unit from the depths of the building and the occasional swish of tires in the street outside.

"Knowing and proving are two different things," Rocco said.

"We don't have a shred of evidence, do we?" Lyon replied.

"Nothing."

"Have the State Police found anything?"

"Nothing."

"Damn it all, Rocco! There's got to be something we can do."

Rocco shook his head. "Like what? Arrest Asa Houston, the most powerful man in this state next to the Governor, take him to the back room for a working over? Let me tell you something, Lyon. My police station doesn't even have a back room. Not that I haven't wanted one from time to time, but my back room is the town library."

"That's a sad state of affairs."

"For what? Police work?"

"No. Our town having a library that small."

"We can't even get a warrant for the bastard. On as little as we've got he'd sue the living be-Jesus out of us."

"Any ideas?"

"No," Rocco said and went back to watching his stop sign. "That is unless you want to go talk to Houston. I can't—I'd be too vulnerable—but you could."

"What would that do?"

"Probably nothing, but a few well-placed remarks might scare the living hell out of him, and could turn up something."

Lyon thought for a moment. "All right."

"Fine," Rocco said, "but be careful as hell."

Lyon sat in his study and looked at the telephone. He felt ill-prepared for this sort of thing and had been postponing the call for several hours.

"I'll call the capitalist pig," Kim said from behind him. "It's a perfect example of a materialistic murder."

"I can hardly convict the man with a copy of Marx," he said.

"Go on, Lyon, make your phone call," Bea said. "I want to hear you call one of the wealthiest men and largest philanthropists in the state a murderer."

"What do you want me to do?" he said crossly.

"I want you to knock it off," she said. "I learned during my first term in the legislature that I couldn't single-handedly change the state. Some things I could do something about, others I could work to improve . . . there were still a lot of gross inequities, poverty, a

164

whole bunch of things, that I couldn't do anything about. I worked toward limited goals I could achieve."

"And the bastard goes free."

"You said you had no evidence against him."

"I would at least like the satisfaction of his knowing that I know what he did."

"Send him an anonymous letter, you know the kind, words clipped from newspapers and mailed from Nova Scotia."

"What ever happened to Battling Beatrice?"

"Sometimes she gets frightened."

"And so do I," Lyon said as he picked up the phone. The receptionist at the Houston Company switched Lyon to Houston's secretary. After some delay Houston was on the phone, his voice dry.

"Yes, Lyon?"

"There had been further developments on the Meyerson matter. I wonder if I might see you?"

"You caught me at a bad time, Wentworth. In two days we have the annual board meetings. I'm looking at my calendar now. How about Tuesday the fourteenth?"

"That's two weeks away."

"As I said, you caught me at a bad time."

"Tomorrow." Lyon was surprised at the authoritative tone of his own voice.

"That's impossible."

"I believe it will be highly informative, Mr. Houston."

There was a pause as Houston considered the proposal. "All right. Tomorrow at my office. Four sharp." The phone went dead in Lyon's hand.

In the late afternoon the two little girls had their tea party on the gable of the barn near the weather vane. They solemnly passed cups and poured tea with great formality. The dark-haired girl laughed, and Lyon's daughter laughed with her. They proceeded to eat scones and tarts, feeding crumbs to teddy bears.

Lyon got slowly up from his desk and the tea party disappeared. He went into the dining room to have a silent meal with his wife.

There was a subdued luxury inherent in the executive wing. The heavy carpet nap muffled footsteps, while indirect lighting gave an almost dreamlike appearance to the paneled hallway. The young receptionist flounced ahead of Lyon as they passed the board room. Asa Houston's office filled the corner of the building next to the board room. The receptionist opened the door to the anteroom and stepped back to let Lyon enter.

Two secretaries clattered at typewriters, one with a transcription listening device in her ear. The older of the two secretaries looked up and smiled.

"Mr. Wentworth?"

"Yes. To see Mr. Houston."

"Mr. Houston had to go over to Building Three for just a few minutes. He's terribly sorry. But if you could wait just a minute or two."

"Yes, thank you. Doesn't Mr. Graves have offices near here? I wonder if I might see him for a moment or two?"

"Of course," she replied and led him down the hallway.

"Thirty-one, thirty-two." He continued with his

count, his face slightly flushed as Lyon examined the office. For its size, and Graves' position in the company, the office had an austere and modest quality. Functional was the best term. The manuals and engineering books in the case were obviously well thumbed, and the desk was a jumble of papers and charts weighted down with a slide rule. The few ornaments on the walls were testimonials from manufacturers and time-study groups, with one large picture showing Graves standing proudly next to the Governor during a ribbon-cutting ceremony at the opening of their automated assembly line in Building Three.

Graves jumped to his feet and quickly toweled his face. "How are you, Wentworth?"

"Fine, just fine. I was hoping I could catch you for a minute before I met with Asa Houston."

"A minute is all you get with me and with Asa." He donned a dress shirt, leaving the knot of his tie halfway down the shirt front. "What can I do for you?"

"Do you know a man named Jonathan Coop?"

"Not offhand."

"He was a government inspector back in the forties."

"Oh, Lord, Wentworth. We've had a hundred inspectors here over the years. Right now I think we've got five permanently assigned to those departments doing government work."

Lyon dropped the line of questioning and bent toward Graves in a conspiratorial manner. "You could be a great help to me. I have an appointment with Houston on a personal matter. If I knew more about the man . . ."

"Nothing confidential about Houston. I've known

him for years. I grew up in this plant. What do you want to know?"

"What kind of man is he?"

"Hell on wheels," Graves said. "Works hard, plays hard. In the old days he could drink any man in the plant under the table. Mean as a Goddamn snake when drunk, but always able to put in a sixteen-hour day."

"He told me about the drinking problem."

"No secret, but that's ancient history. Asa hasn't had a drink in fifteen years. Gave it up one day and that was that. Wouldn't be surprised if his wife wasn't the one who was instrumental in that."

"She's a lovely woman," Lyon said.

"Cool as they come and smarter than most. They met here, you know."

"No, I didn't know."

"Yep, Helen was the first woman engineer we ever hired. I was against it in those days. Hell, I never knew they had women engineers then, but she was good. Maybe that's why Asa decided to give her special treatment and then fell for her."

Graves carefully rolled up a large sheaf of blueprints and tucked them under his arm. "Anything else, Wentworth? I think I've found the answer to an engineering bug over at the automated plant that's been bothering me for days." He reverently ran his fingers along the edges of the prints.

"No, thank you very much."

Lyon started down the hallway toward Houston's office and on impulse stepped into the adjoining board room. It was as he recalled. There was a door from the board room directly into Houston's private office.

The door closed silently behind him, and he moved quickly through the room. Floor-length windows, shuttered by heavy drapes, ran along two walls. The remaining walls, paneled in heavy oak were lined with built-in bookshelves, a bar, and doors to the board-room secretaries' office, and a third door to a private bath and sauna.

At the apex of the room, near the window corner, sat a massive desk with three side chairs. Away from the desk and arranged in a comfortable semi-circle were divans and easy chairs separated by a glass-topped coffee table. It was a tasteful and masculine room; silver-plated parts manufactured by the company were set at odd angles on sculpture stanchions and gave the appearance of modernistic art. The room was an extension of power, decorated in a calculated manner to exhibit success, with the furnishings staged so that the desk's occupant would dominate the setting.

There were only a few items on the broad desk top: a gold pen and an appointment calendar at the front, with a copy of the company's financial statement placed next to a legal pad. A row of buttons, inlaid in the desk top, were easily accessible to whoever occupied the chair.

He picked up the annotated appointment calendar. His own name was down for 4 P.M., a Roger Hackman at 4:45. Lyon flipped through the pages containing appointments for the next two weeks, and then replaced the calendar in its proper place.

He pressed one of the inlaid buttons and the drape behind him began to open. Pressing the button counterpart, the drapes shut on noiseless runners. The second button in line caused a quiet click from the office doors, and he realized that they had automatically locked. He unlocked the doors by depressing the next button.

In actuality the room revealed little about its occupant. That it had been consciously designed and staged was obvious. It would be here that Houston would deal with his company officers, bankers and investors. The books in the shelves were bound in uniform expensive leather and appeared unread. The objects and the artifacts were impersonal.

He knew little about this man and earlier in the day had gone to the library to read old newspaper files. Last year, after a particularly large gift to the orchestra, the paper had run a Sunday feature article on Asa Houston. Asa Houston: wealthy industrialist and philanthropist. Born to a poor family, he was a self educated and self-made man of the old school. Starting as an apprentice tool and diemaker, he had started the Houston Company in 1940 on three thousand dollars of borrowed capital. The war, government loans for expansion, and a shrewd talent for negotiating cost-plus contracts had made him a wealthy man.

Lyon sat behind the desk and slowly opened the center drawer. The drawer's contents were as neat as the remainder of the room. A few file folders with typed headings, a slide rule, sharpened pencils. Resting on a clean white cloth was a 38-caliber Smith and Wesson revolver.

"Do you like my toys, Mr. Wentworth?"

Asa Houston stood by the door with a half-smile curling one side of his face. The door slammed behind him as he strode toward Lyon and took the revolver from the drawer.

"This is a gun, Mr. Wentworth. This gun is not for plinking; it is not for shooting snakes. It is kept for the specific purpose for which it was designed . . . to shoot people."

Lyon stood up, his face flushed, and mumbled, "Sorry."

"You should be. There are unpleasant names for what you have been doing. Now, will you sit down or would you prefer my desk?"

Lyon came out from behind the desk and sat in a side chair. Houston replaced the revolver in the drawer, seated himself at the desk and looked expectantly at Lyon. "You should have stayed behind the desk, Mr. Wentworth. The man behind the desk has a decided advantage."

"I didn't come for advantage."

"Perhaps you came to thank me for the small honorarium the company sent you . . . or wasn't it enough for your services?"

Their eyes met. "Exactly why are you here?" Houston continued.

"I've just returned from Florida. As I explained on the phone, I was able to develop some information that might be of interest to you."

"Yes?"

How do you start? Lyon thought. How do you tell a man you think he killed three people? Houston leaned forward, not tense, not nervous . . .

171

"Yes, Mr. Wentworth?"

Lyon told him about the Florida trip, the breakfast on the boat with Jonathan Coop, and Coop's admission regarding the passing of inferior parts. Houston listened without comment, making no inquiries, asking for no additional details. His eyes and posture revealed nothing to Lyon. When Lyon finished there was a pause between them.

"I take it," Houston said, "that you're here to accuse me of bribing a government official."

"And more."

"That I had a motive for killing the Meyerson family?"

"Yes." Lyon handed Coop's affidavit across the desk. Houston read it and looked up.

"This paper isn't notarized or witnessed," he said. "It's a worthless document."

"It's in his handwriting. I can witness."

"I'm afraid that's not quite adequate." Asa Houston slowly tore the affidavit into neat squares and dropped them into the waste basket. Both men watched them flutter into the container.

"That's only a copy," Lyon said.

"Of course. My gesture was symbolic. What do you want, Wentworth? Like Coop—money? Not that it really matters."

"I want to know about the Meyersons."

"You conveniently shot Bull Martin. That should be satisfaction enough for you."

"Bull didn't kill them, at least all of them. I'm sure of that."

"You seem to operate on some sort of mystical process of elimination. In other words, if Bull didn't kill them, I did?"

"You had a motive."

"You have absolutely nothing. There isn't a particle of evidence in anything you say or hint."

"There's always something somewhere, Mr. Houston. Even thirty years after, there's something that can fill in the details, and I will find it. I have a few leads, and I promise you I will find it."

Houston regarded him reflectively. "You might at that. You've done very well so far."

"If that shipment of parts in 1943 had been rejected by the Army, you would have gone under. I am sure we can reconstruct that."

"You might. I'm not sure how long certain records are retained by banks, or by the government. Knowing the government, I'm sure they have purchase requisitions going back to the Revolutionary War. That part is true, Wentworth. Houston Company in 1943 was on shaky ground. Everything we had or could beg, borrow or steal had gone into expansion and purchase of material. The rejection of that shipment would have toppled the house of cards. Yes, I did pay off Coop. Yes, I did bribe a government official. I'll deny that, out of this room and forever, I'll deny that. And I might point out that the statute of limitations has run out."

"So I've been told."

"In those days our quality control was primitive. It was a bad batch and Meyerson knew it."

"And you killed him."

"I intended to reach him in other ways. He was a

stubborn little guy, but I would have found a way. There's always a way."

"I don't think he would have taken your money."

"Oh, no. I tried that first. No, he was quite stubborn about that, had this thing about the Nazis, a just war and all that sort of thing. But I had found a way. He had relatives in a concentration camp. I was working out a method to obtain their release and smuggle them to Switzerland."

"Is that possible?"

"Anything is possible with enough money. I would have taken care of Meyerson in my own manner."

"What about his family?"

"I had nothing to do with that."

"Someone did," Lyon said.

Asa Houston got up from the desk and crossed the room to where the silver parts stood. He ran a hand along the edge of one of the finely machined pieces. "Yes, someone did," he said.

"The information on the pay-off is enough to ruin you," Lyon said.

"My word carries a bit of weight in this community, in the whole state in fact. My record is excellent, a career without blemish. We don't manufacture poor parts anymore. We're quite good. I don't make the same mistake twice. In 1943 I had to. It was a question of simple survival."

"For you. Not the others."

"Would you believe me if I said I didn't kill them?"

"No."

"Because there's no statute of limitations on murder?"

"Partially."

"Nevertheless, I would prefer that none of this . . . this unpleasantness were published. I can make life awfully difficult for you, Mr. Wentworth."

"I am sure you can."

"Much more than you can possibly dream. Shall we start with your wife's political career? Hardly difficult to stop that. The refusal by the State Committee to endorse her, the refusal of her own district to renominate her, the extensive backing of a counter candidate."

"I know you can do that."

"And your publishers. How will they take to having a children's author who's arrested for indecent exposure?"

"I will tie you directly into this."

"I prefer to handle it my own way."

"Three people are dead. . . ."

"I said drop it!"

"No."

"Then I will neutralize you, Wentworth. Do you understand that?" Asa Houston returned to the desk. "Let me spell it out. Even if I didn't kill them, even if I can't be prosecuted for pay-offs made thirty years ago, I have no intention of having the slightest smear against the Houston name. I've spent too many years building a reputation in this state to have you destroy it. I made millions and I gave millions and no old ghosts are going to take that from me."

Lyon leaned over the desk, fingers clenched on the smooth surface. The musculature of his arms and legs seemed to have dissolved as an all-persuasive weakness surrounded him, the immediate forerunner of large doses of adrenaline coursing through his body.

"What about the little girl?" Lyon yelled.

"The hell with the little girl," Houston said impatiently.

Lyon's fist glanced off the other man's cheekbone. His clawing hands reached across the desk and grasped the lapels of Houston's coat. The immediate leverage pulled Houston halfway across the desk before he regained his balance and backed away.

Houston's hands reached for the buttons, and Lyon dimly heard the sound of an alarm, and then Houston's fist smashed into his nose and he fell back. They were in the center of the room grappling as the guards rushed through the door.

The secretary stood with her hands at her face ready to scream as the two security guards grabbed Lyon and pulled him away from Asa Houston.

"Get that Goddamn idiot out of here," Houston screamed. "Get him out and keep him out!"

"You want the police, Mr. Houston?" the guard asked as he pinned Lyon's arms.

"No. Just throw him out!"

"Come on, duck butter," the large guard said as they dragged Lyon from the office.

In the hallway, out of sight of the secretaries, they pushed Lyon against the wall. A billy-club dug into his stomach and a knee into his groin, and then he felt another crack against his nose. He heard them dimly as they dragged him to the parking lot.

"Come on, sweetheart, let's go bye-bye."

Lyon lay, his head against the steering wheel, miles from the Houston factory. Blood dripped from his nose and formed a small pool on his pants leg and then ran in a small rivulet down to the car mat.

He held his handkerchief against the nose and blinked his eyes to clear the tearing. He climbed slowly from the car and began to walk up the hill.

Nine

He sat on top of the hill with his back propped against his daughter's tombstone and thought about what sort of person he was becoming.

The cemetery was in Middleburg, only a few miles from the house. Perhaps because of the difficult struggle for life in the early days, the first settlers had picked a large hill in the center of town, truly the choicest location, as the site for their burial ground. It must have been a yearning on their parts, an expression of faith that the hereafter would be preferable to the mortal coil, and therefore deserved the most scenic area in the town limits. His daughter was buried here for that reason, and also because Wentworths had been buried here for 150 years.

Lyon was a Unitarian. A faith that some chided was a little about God, a little about religion, and mostly about Boston. He didn't know if he believed in an afterlife, and never thought of his daughter in those terms, although in some mystical way she sat specterlike at his elbow when he created his books for an audience of one—one who would always be eight years old.

It wasn't the beating by Houston's security force that bothered him. It was the all-consuming anger that had made him hit another man, something he hadn't done since grade school days. And yet, in the light of recent events, the action wasn't unusual. In the past weeks he had killed one man, threatened to throw a dying man's medication into the sea and physically attacked another man.

His past life had been dedicated to an artistic orderliness; even the few years in the Army had fallen into that category, and, except for an isolated example or two, his service as an intelligence officer had been an intellectual game.

Did it matter that Houston might be the creator of the ancient grave? Was justice, whatever that was, served by his admission or nonadmission of guilt? Lyon knew the answer.

His anger and attack had been directed as much at his own helplessness in the situation as against Houston. He was at a loss in which direction to go—and yet he couldn't drop the matter and let it fade into an insignificant memory.

He tried to order his thoughts. In one sense they had come far; they had established identities and tied the Houston Company into the murders; and now it was impossible to disengage the relationship of the dead Meyersons from the bribery of the government inspector.

She started up the hill. When she saw him her pace quickened. Her hair blew in the wind and her eyes squinted slightly against the sun as she looked toward him, and Lyon loved his wife very much. She was now almost running toward him, her legs flashing in the sun; her knees and hips had changed little from those of the girl he had married.

She was out of breath when she reached the top of the hill. The squint faded as she seemed to be about to say something but instead sat next to him on the grass. After a few moments she turned toward him. "WE'VE BEEN WORRIED ABOUT YOU."

"I'm O.K."

"Rocco called the Houston Company and found out what happened. Are you sure you're all right?"

"Sure."

"You've been up here all night. THAT'S A KOOKY THING TO DO," she said and seemed to regret it instantly. "I'm sorry, I know you're upset."

"I wanted to kill him, Bea. If I'd been stronger, or trained, or had had a weapon, I might have. At that moment I wanted to kill him."

"You never will again, Lyon."

"I wouldn't have thought so, but recently . . ."

"No, not him. Not ever again," she said. "Asa Houston is dead."

Rocco's cruiser was at the cemetery gate, and as Lyon and Bea got into the rear seat Lyon's right leg began to tremble and his hands to shake. He hadn't been able to assimilate Houston's death—the velocity of events was beginning to take its toll, reality taking on a strange tinge that gave a dream quality to ordinary and mundane things. His nerves were stretched to an unhealthy tautness.

Rocco drove a few miles to a small restaurant off the main roads. Inside, the large man took command of the ordering—heavy drinks immediately, followed by steaks. Lyon drank his double sherry, and as the warmth spread through his body the trembling began to subside. He exhaled slowly and leaned back. "All right," he said. "I guess I'm ready for it. What happened to Houston?"

Rocco pulled the notebook from his breast pocket. "You want it exact?"

"Exact."

"This morning while Bea and I were chasing over half the state trying to find you, we caught the bulletin over the car radio. I called downtown and got some of the details from a friend of mine."

Beatrice put her hand on Lyon's. Lyon brushed his forehead with his free hand. "I don't know what to say. It's too fast. Details, Rocco. Details."

"This morning at twenty-two minutes past ten Asa Houston shot himself in his office."

"How do you know he shot himself?"

For a moment Rocco looked tired and then continued in a factual monotone. "At exactly ten twenty-two this morning a shot was heard from Asa Houston's office. A foremen's meeting was going on in the board room next door; they broke open the door and found him behind the desk, the gun next to his body."

"His own gun?" Lyon asked. "The one from the desk?"

"Yes. Anyway, that's about it, except they found a message on his office recorder. A classic suicide message."

"I don't believe it," Lyon said.

"OH, FOR GOD'S SAKE, LYON," Bea said. "Come off it, really."

Rocco turned to Beatrice. "He means he can't believe in a different sense, Bea. Too much has happened; it's hard to realize that it's all over."

"That's not at all what I meant," Lyon said. "I don't think Asa Houston killed himself."

"People do it all the time, old buddy."

"Let's take him home," Bea said and attempted a laugh.

Rocco leaned forward in his best professional manner, and for a moment Lyon felt that he'd run a stop sign and the Chief was preparing a lecture. "Now listen, old friend, and listen good. Here's what happened. You saw Houston yesterday afternoon; you obviously got to him or he wouldn't have reacted. He knew you couldn't be kept out of the way indefinitely, that eventually you'd be back with additional evidence."

"I hinted that to him."

"Right. Now, he's already shook because we traced the bodies and linked them to Houston Company. You've tracked down the government inspector; you're hot on his trail. He can't bear up under it; he spends a restless night, can't see any way out, and this morning . . . whacko. It's all over. Now, doesn't that make sense?"

"Yes, it makes a lot of sense. Houston was afraid of us, arranged for Bull Martin to pull his deal, knew I saw Coop in Florida . . ."

"A question of time."

"We didn't have a damn thing, Rocco. Not really. You know that, I know that and he knew that."

"Did he? What about his guilt all those years? Why do you think he was the state's biggest philanthropist? He'd created an image, and you were about to destroy it."

"What more do you want, Lyon?" Beatrice said. "A dozen people saw Houston go into his office, thirty people heard the shot, and within minutes twenty of those were in the office where Houston was dead by his own gun. No one else was there."

"And a message on the recording machine," Rocco said.

"I'd like to hear that message," Lyon said. "I'd like very much to hear it."

Rocco Herbert pushed the police car to seventy on the deserted Interstate as Lyon clutched the edge of his seat. As he glanced down at the floorboards, the sight of Rocco's leg in a cast did not reassure him at all.

"Will the Hartford police cooperate?" he asked.

"Yes, as a courtesy, but if we release anything to the news media they'll have my head."

"That's understandable."

Police headquarters on Morgan Street in downtown Hartford nestled underneath the raised junction of two Interstate highways on one side and a large plaza and office complex on the other. The interconnected buildings were a maze of diverse architecture, the front section a relatively modern edifice, connected to an older portion containing the courts and offices.

Rocco slid the cruiser into the official lot and led Lyon through a maze of corridors to a small office.

Detective Sergeant Michael Pasquale met Rocco with a jab to the solar plexus. Rocco countered with a bear hug that lifted the slim detective several feet into the air and made him gasp for breath.

"Put me down, you half-guinea bastard," the raised man finally managed to gasp.

"You're getting thinner, Pat. What's the matter, not getting enough off the pad these days?"

"Screw you. If I had half a grain of sense I'd be in a cushy spot like yours, laying half the housewives in town."

"Only the ones under seventy."

"With them on top, you big bastard."

They went into the small office. The room was bare, the peeling walls partially covered by a large map of the city, with a battered desk and two wooden folding chairs for visitors.

"You got the tape?" Rocco asked.

"I got it for the time being, but for Christ's sake don't breathe a word about hearing it. The Houston family would have my badge."

The detective pulled a small cassette player from the desk and inserted a cartridge. He positioned the tape and looked at them expectantly. "Ready for the command performance?" They nodded and he pressed the play button.

The tape hummed for a few moments, and then they could hear the rustle of papers and the unmistakable voice. Lyon knew it was Houston's voice, but the quiet monotone surprised him.

"I have come to the end," the tape intoned. "There are few alternatives left, and I am taking the only course of action open to me. Everything is in order and the lawyers will know where to look." The voice stopped. Faint indescribable sounds could be heard, then the opening of a drawer. Lyon could imagine Houston's hand reaching into the center drawer and withdrawing the pistol. The drawer closed. Again there was silence on the tape until the faint click of the revolver's action, followed by the shot.

The sound filled the room, and, although expected,

it startled the three of them. There were several seconds of silence again before the muffled sound of someone beating on a door, and then complete silence as the tape reached the end of the spool.

"How do you reconstruct it?" Lyon asked.

"We would have eventually, but his secretary noticed that the recorder light was still on. We played it back and got this."

"What's on the rest of the tape?" Rocco asked.

"Absolutely nothing of interest. Letters he dictated, memoranda and other routine stuff. I had the secretaries listen to it also. They told me that there was nothing out of the ordinary."

"How do you reconstruct it?" Lyon asked.

"What you hear is what we got," the short detective replied. "No reason to feel otherwise. At approximately ten o'clock he locked his door, which is not a particularly unusual thing for him to do, they tell me. He was a real bug for privacy. He was despondent, mumbled those few remarks into the recorder and then shot himself. My God, you heard what happened on the tape."

"What's the pounding after the shot?" Lyon asked.

"We're not sure if that's his secretary from the outer office or the foremen next door in the board room. It's up to the coroner, of course, but my report is as conclusive as I can make it. Self-inflicted gunshot wound. How could it be anything else?"

At nine the following morning Lyon Wentworth slowed his small car at the security gate of the Houston Company. As he waved to the guard and attempted to accelerate again, he was forced to slam on

the brakes as the rail gate closed in front of him. Th
guard approached the car.

"The plant is closed for the day in honor of M
Houston," the guard mumbled.

Lyon saw that the large parking lots were almo
empty, that the broad expanse of asphalt usual
filled with cars, pick-up trucks and campers was no
empty, except for an occasional vehicle inexplicab
parked in various parts of the two large lots. Four ca
were parked directly in front of the administratio
building.

"I see that there's someone in the administratio
building," Lyon said.

"I'm sorry, Mr. Wentworth. We're closed."

There was an unusual harshness to the guard
voice, a return to police authority from this heretofor
friendly man.

"It's really quite important," Lyon said.

"I'm sorry, Mr. Wentworth. I'm trying to make it a
easy as possible on you. My orders are never to le
you in here. I can't."

The guard stood directly in Lyon's path, and out
side of running the man down, Lyon had no access t
the plant. A flash of memory concerning all the pri
vate investigators he'd read about flicked through hi
mind. A Sam Spade would slip the intransigent guard
a few dollars and quickly speed to the administration
building. Lyon patted his side pocket . . . he didn'
have a few dollars. He didn't even have his wallet.

Parking at a nearby diner he scrounged through the
glove compartment and eventually discovered tw
dimes. He dialed Rocco's number and explained the
problem.

"No way," the large man's voice boomed back at him over the phone. "Go home. It's over, man. Over."

"You want the nomination for town clerk at the town committee meeting next week?"

"You make it sound like you're asking if I still have relatives in Germany. That's lousy and rotten."

"I feel lousy and rotten."

"Pasquale will never buy it." His voice dropped to an almost solicitous tone. "I'm sorry I ever got you into this."

Lyon looked down at the single dime in the palm of his hand. "I'm at the diner on Elm Street. Hurry up, will you? I only have enough money for one cup of coffee."

Rocco reluctantly agreed, said he'd phone Detective Pasquale and they'd pick Lyon up in forty-five minutes. However, he found he was wrong. Coffee was fifteen cents a cup. He waited in his car and read the owner's manual completely through several times before Rocco and Pasquale arrived in an unmarked city police car.

Pat Pasquale jumped from the car and grimly approached Lyon. "Listen, Wentworth. Your big buddy here has talked me into this, but if these people should complain . . . if word gets back to the police commissioner, it'll be my ass—and if it's my ass and I'm back on the beat . . . you'll never drive the streets of Hartford again."

"I want to express my appreciation to both of you for your cooperation," Lyon said as he got into the back of the police car.

"I have only myself to blame," Rocco said, shaking his head.

The security guard recognized Pat as they ap
proached and waved them through with a salute
They barked to a quick stop in front of the adminis
tration building, Pat leaping from the car as if h
were breaking up a holdup in progress. Rocco, com
plete with cane, eased his bulk from the seat and to
ward the stairs. The two policemen turned toward
Lyon.

"You coming?" Rocco asked.

"There aren't any inside door handles back here,"
Lyon said.

Pat released the rear doors and they entered the
building. The reception area of the administration
building was large, the walls covered with photo
graphs of various plant operations, and display case
throughout the room exhibited several of the factory'
completed products. The receptionist's glass booth
was empty. A security captain lumbered from a side
door to meet them and pump Pat's hand.

"Thought you was finished yesterday, Pat."

"Routine. A few loose ends before my final report.
How's it going, Bill? Keeping up the pace?"

"Hell, at least the hours are regular. That's better'n
the force, and don't knock the excitement. Last year I
caught a creep in the ladies' room."

Pat introduced them to the security captain, identifying Rocco as the chief of the Murphysville police
and, without exactly stating what, made hints that
Lyon had some sort of official capacity.

"Where were you when they found the body, Captain?" Lyon asked.

"Right back here in the monitor room. That's where
our closed circuit TV cameras are watched. I got an

emergency signal from Miss Reed—that's Houston's number one secretary—and I was up there about the time the foremen broke the door in."

"Was there anyone in the room besides Houston?" Rocco asked.

"Nope. The foremen went in, and I was right after them. I'll swear to it."

"Who had keys to his office doors besides Mr. Houston?" Lyon asked.

"Just me," the captain replied. "Not another person in the world. Mr. Houston was a bug on security. You should see the equipment we've got—out of this world."

"Where's your key now?" Pat said.

The guard captain pulled a keyring from his pocket. The ring was securely attached to his belt by a small chain. He flipped through the ring quickly before selecting and holding out a slim key. "Here it is. Never left me."

"I won't stay in the same room with that man," Miss Florence Reed said while pointing an accusatory finger at Lyon. "If it wasn't for what he did, frightening Mr. Houston and carrying on . . . this wouldn't have happened." She turned away, a handkerchief to her eyes.

"We're here on official business, Miss Reed," Pat said in a somber tone. "You could be of help."

"I wouldn't even be here today if Mr. Graves hadn't called and asked me to come and help get things together for the board meeting." She sat at her desk and stared disconsolately at the file folders piled before her. "But I find it so difficult to concentrate."

189

She was an attractive but sexless woman in her mid forties, immaculately groomed, the type of woman who wore her glasses across her breast on a thin dark band. Her attire was almost always white blouse and dark, well-tailored suit.

She let them in Houston's office and went back to her desk to look blankly at her file folders. They closed the door softly and walked around the large office.

The room appeared undisturbed, exactly as Lyon had seen it less than forty-eight hours ago. Any reminders of the death of Houston had been removed. The desk was shiny, the appointment pad and legal pad still neatly aligned on its surface.

"Do you know why in hell we're here?" Pat said to Rocco.

"No," the large man replied and turned to Lyon. "Why do you think he didn't kill himself?"

Lyon crossed to the desk and picked up the appointment pad. "I'm not sure," he said, "except that I know that the man I talked to in this office wouldn't have. He wasn't the sort of man who'd turn a gun on himself the next morning."

"Bullshit!" the Hartford detective said. "I've investigated maybe fifty suicides. They're all kinds of people, successful, unsuccessful, rich, poor, you name it. Who knows why someone really decides to take the big step?"

"Wouldn't you say there are certain patterns?" Lyon continued. "And I'm speaking now of the serious ones, not the pill-takers or wrist-slashers, the ones who put a gun to their head. Aren't there patterns?"

"Of course," the detective replied. "Suicides fall into

two categories: the neurotic cry for help, those who don't really expect to die, but sometimes are a little overzealous and do; and the serious ones. Like, say, the ones who put the gun to the head—that's serious."

Rocco took the appointment pad and flipped through it. "What's the pattern?"

"Like Houston," Pat said. "Well dressed, his desk neat, his note on the recorder, 'see the lawyers,' it said, everything neatly packaged and then—bam."

"A considered course of action," Lyon said.

"Exactly. Probably as precise as the way he ran his business."

Lyon took the appointment calendar from Rocco. "Why would a man in the last few minutes of his life make appointments as far as two weeks away, some the same afternoon?"

"What do you mean?" the detective asked.

"I saw the future appointments," Rocco said. "But who knows when they were made unless we check them all out."

"I remember," Lyon said. He sat at the desk and quickly began to write names, dates and times on the legal pad. Finished, he handed the sheet to Rocco. "When I was in this office the other day I looked at this pad. Here's a list of appointments he had at that time . . . compare them to the list now on the calendar."

The detective and Rocco sat on a divan and compared the lists. "There's five additional appointments," Rocco finally said.

"That doesn't mean a damn thing," the detective said impatiently. "Houston probably got twenty calls a day from people trying to see him. On that last morning he found it easier to agree than to put them off. Out of force of habit he made the note on the calendar."

"Possibly," Lyon said. "Let's ask Miss Reed."

Florence Reed, eyes red-rimmed, followed Rocco back into the room and stood uncomfortably near the desk. Her hands twisted a small handkerchief until one bony finger made another gesture toward Lyon. "Does that man have to be here?" she asked.

"Yes, he does," Rocco said. "Mrs. Reed, you . . ."

"It's Miss."

"Yes. Miss Reed, you worked for Mr. Houston for several years?"

"Twenty years, as his private secretary for fifteen. He was a wonderful man."

"You were here when Mr. Wentworth and Mr. Houston had their altercation?"

"I certainly was."

"What happened after that?" Rocco asked.

"Just a moment, please." She went quickly back to her desk and returned with an office diary. Efficiently she flipped through the pages, the return to professionalism seeming to grant her greater self-control. She read from her diary in a monotone. "He . . . Mr. Wentworth, arrived at 4 P.M. Mr. Houston had an emergency call to Building Three and I asked . . . him . . . to wait. Mr. Houston returned at 4:08. At 4:40 Mr. Wentworth was removed from the office. There were a great many people in the office for a while, then at five Mr. Roger Hackman came for his appointment. Mr. Houston left for home at 5:45."

"Who's Mr. Hackman?" Lyon asked.

Florence Reed looked at Lyon without answering

until asked the same question by Rocco Herbert. "I don't know," she finally said.

"You were his private secretary for fifteen years and yet don't know this man?" Rocco's voice had turned to authority.

Florence Reed seemed truly flustered. "I . . . I don't know. I almost always know who he has a meeting with, but a week ago, when he made that appointment, I asked who Mr. Hackman was affiliated with and he wouldn't answer."

"You're positive he left at 5:45?" Pat said.

"I am absolutely positive. I never left before Mr. Houston did."

"What about the next morning?" Rocco pressed quickly.

"Mr. Houston arrived at the office at 8:45. Debbie, that's the other girl in the office, served him coffee and a sweet roll. He met with Mr. Graves for ten minutes, and at 9:15 Mrs. Houston arrived."

"Mrs. Houston?"

"Yes, she stayed until around ten. Mr. Houston must have locked the doors after she left."

Lyon looked at the appointment pad. "Then between 9:05 and 9:15 and from 10:00 until he died, Mr. Houston made five appointments."

"I don't know," she replied. "I suppose so."

Lyon handed her the list of new appointments. "Can you tell me who these people are?"

She looked at the list for a moment. "The appointment scheduled for eleven that morning was Mr. Giles, that's his personal attorney. Mr. Houston used Mr. Giles for his personal work or his confidential matters. The next one, Mr. Henderson, is our vice-president in charge of sales; Mr. Qunlaye is a trust officer at the bank; Mr. Williams is Mr. Houston's private accountant. And then Mr. Hackman again."

"I'm interested in the recording machine, Mrs. Reed," Lyon said.

"It's Miss. What is it you want to know?"

"Did Mr. Houston often record his letters and memos?"

"Constantly. He had a set in his car, his home, and here, just like all the executives do. We record all the board meetings and many of the important committee meetings. Mr. Houston was very meticulous about accuracy."

"I have a question, Miss Reed," the detective said. "As I understand it, Mrs. Houston left at ten that morning."

"That is correct."

"And no one went in or came out after that?"

"No one."

"You weren't away from your desk during that time, for coffee, the powder room, anything?"

"Debbie and I were both in the outer office until we heard the shot. Neither of us left."

"Thank you very much," Rocco said. She fled the room back to her desk.

Lyon walked slowly to the desk. It hadn't changed from his first examination. Pushing the drapes aside he inspected the windows. The large panes of glass fit securely into the building frame without any opening mechanism. "We don't know if someone was hiding in the bathroom," Lyon said.

"I thought of that possibility," Pat said tiredly. "Six

company foremen tell me they looked. Right after they busted the door down, they looked. There's a dozen witnesses that swear no one was in the room when the shot was heard except Asa Houston. Period. Now, you can fool around all you want with appointment pads and all that crap, but let me tell you, buddy, there ain't no way."

"The gun was his?"

"Of course. Registered and with his prints on it."

Lyon sat at the desk. He placed his arms along the sides of the desk and then slowly clasped them together.

"What in hell's he doing?" Pat said to Rocco.

"He thinks a lot," Rocco said.

"God spare me." The detective flung himself on the divan and put his feet on the coffee table. "He's thinking. I'll be back busting queers on Sission Street."

Lyon picked up the tape recorder microphone. "The mike was here on the desk?" he asked Pat.

The detective glanced over his shoulder. "Yep."

Lyon opened the center drawer of the desk and picked up an imaginary revolver. He placed the imaginary barrel against his temple. "Like this?" he asked Pat.

"Yeah, but not quite so close. He musta' held it out a few inches."

"Where was the gun found and how was the body positioned?"

The little detective jumped to his feet and crossed to the desk. "Are you almost through?"

"Almost. Where exactly were they?" Lyon asked again.

"The gun was by the chair, maybe three feet to the right side. He must have dropped it when he fell."

"He fell to the floor."

"You don't know what the poor guy looked like. That's a powerful little weapon at that range."

Lyon leaned back in the chair and closed his eyes until Rocco shook his shoulder. "I know you're tired, old buddy," Rocco said, "but this is not a flophouse."

"Are we through?" Pat asked.

"Through," Lyon said.

"Thank God."

As they marched single file toward the outer office Pat opened the door with a flourish and stepped aside with a mock bow. Miss Reed was still contemplating her folders.

"I'd like to thank you for your cooperation, Miss Reed," Rocco said. "If you can think of anything else that happened that morning, would you please call Detective Pasquale?"

"Of course," she replied absently as the men started for the door. "Although I can't understand why she was crying."

They turned. "Who was crying?" Rocco asked.

"Why, Mrs. Houston," she said. "When she left the office that morning she was crying. She tried to hide it, but I've known her for years, and she was crying."

Ten

Hand in hand, Bea and Lyon walked across the firm sand at water's edge. A cool sea breeze whipped her hair back and eddied the rushes beyond the beach. They wore identical light tan jackets and white tennis shoes.

The empty beach and expanse of sea gave them an illusion of great privacy, a panacea for their recent acrimony. Ahead, two little girls danced at water's edge, rushing toward the slight rippling surf, then back again laughing. Lyon blinked and turned away; when he turned back the children were still there.

Bea gripped his hand tightly and waved to the little girls. The children waved back and then ran off behind the dunes. "They're there . . . they really are," Bea said.

Lyon coughed, pinched the bridge of his nose and smiled at his wife. "There are times when I wonder," he said.

They walked on, their footprints making slight indentations in the packed sand. "Over there," Bea said and led him by the hand toward a protected rift in the dunes. They sat in the sand, their shoulders touching, and looked toward the sea. The small semi-circle, surrounded by dunes, opened to the sea, and they lay back against the side. "Hungry?" she asked.

"Not yet. In a little while." He placed the small rucksack at their feet and kissed her on the forehead. Protected from the winds, they were warmed by the sun as barely perceptible water sounds swept across the sand. They had known the Cape wouldn't be crowded during early spring, and with spent emotions had wordlessly driven half the night toward their secluded destination.

Bea's shallow breathing told Lyon that she'd fallen asleep and he laid his jacket across her. They had spent their honeymoon near here, which made it a fit place to return to for the nursing of recent wounds. The previous night's arguments surrounded him.

"IT'S OVER, OVER, OVER WITH!" she had screamed.

"No, damn it! Not yet."

"It's wrong and all tied up with Sandra. You're trying to expiate some imaginary sin by this obsession. The murder of a little girl thirty years ago gives you nightmares about your own child. We had almost forgotten, Lyon. It was gone and didn't hurt so much anymore."

"I hadn't forgotten," he said aloud.

Beatrice sat up on the sand. "What did you say?"

"Nothing. I'm sorry I disturbed you. You know, I think I am hungry now." He opened the rucksack and took out sandwiches, hard-boiled eggs and a small bottle of wine. "In fact, I'm starved."

They ate quietly and drank small cups of Rhine wine. Lyon sensed her looking at him. "We could adopt a child," she said. "I've wanted to for years. I could even stay in the legislature—it only meets a few months a year—and I'd have plenty of time to care for her."

"I'm not ready for that yet."

He knew what his books were, and as long as he created children's fantasies she was there. He wrote

198

them for her, to her, and because of that she still existed for him.

"There are so many children who need a home," she said.

He put his arm on her shoulder. "Please . . . let's walk some more."

In late day when they approached the cottage at water's edge they were as tired as they wanted to be. The man in the shadows of the small porch propped one foot on the porch railing as he leaned the chair against the wall. Lyon and Bea were at the porch steps, still oblivious to his presence when he spoke.

"I think I know how it was done," Rocco Herbert said.

"Oh, my God, he's haunting us," Bea said and fled into the cottage.

"How in hell did you find us? No one knew we were coming here," Lyon said.

"Put out an APB to locate a material witness, and I've certainly given you enough traffic tickets to know your marker number."

Lyon sat in the chair next to Rocco. "I'm not interested. I've half-promised Bea that I'm through with it."

"Can't blame you. You've had enough grief over this mess."

The descending sun darkened the water before them. Wordlessly, Bea served drinks and disappeared back into the cottage. Occasionally Rocco shifted his injured leg with a quiet grunt, while Lyon looked across the dunes.

"All right," Lyon finally said. "I can't stand it. How was it done?"

* * *

The small brass plate on the front of the brownstone house near the state capitol told the passing world that Saxon, Giles, Renfrow and Hoppelwite, Attorneys at Law, occupied the building. Immediately inside the door a claw-leg table with highly polished top supported the tired elbows of an elderly man.

"May I help you, sir," the older man said, his rheumy eyes seeming to stare through Lyon disdainfully toward the elbow patches on his suit jacket.

"I have an appointment with Mr. Giles. My name is Wentworth."

He followed the ancient retainer up the narrow, winding marble staircase to the second floor. Old prints and maps decorated the hallway, while similar doors opened into antique-filled offices.

The office of Thomas G. Giles II clearly had the hallmark of a very senior partner in the firm. Its corner location overviewing the park and state capitol, and the fine clean-lined early American antiques gave off an aura of subliminal ostentation. The office occupant was a ruddy-faced man of fifty with a shock of carefully groomed white hair. A well-manicured hand with Harvard class ring was extended.

"Wentworth!" Giles said. "Farmington Prep—Lacrosse—Captain 1948."

"Dobbie Giles, you were captain when I was a freshman." Lyon slipped easily into the almost-forgotten, but never-lost, mantle of "Old Yankee." They laughed as long ago days on sunny playing fields assumed vibrancy and the dire enemies of Choate, Petty and Andover assumed reality again. A nagging thought concerning the old adage that the battles of the British Empire were won on the playing fields of Eton came to mind, and as Lyon viewed the pretentious man before him, he felt he knew why the Empire had been lost.

Giles settled back in his seat. ". . . and then Harvard, V-12 of course during the war." He paused as his mental shift was made. "You wanted to see me concerning the Houston matter."

"Yes, I did. I've been indirectly involved with the Houston Company on a matter, and his death . . ."

"Bothers you. Off the record, I don't mind telling you that it does me too. Not in character at all. There's really not much I can help you with—the attorney-client relationship still exists."

"Of course, Dobbie, but a little information off the record would be of invaluable assistance."

"That might depend on what it is. Exactly what did you want to know?"

"Why did Houston want to see you?"

Dobbie Giles tapped a slim gold pencil on the desk. "He said it was urgent, so much so that I canceled two previous engagements to make room to see him. He did say that our meeting would concern two matters."

"Can you tell me what they are?"

"No, not completely; but off the record, Lyon . . . one concerned breaking the employment contract of a highly placed officer in the company."

"The other?"

"This is really off the record, and if it gets out I'll deny it. It was a domestic relations problem. That's all I can say."

"Do you know who Roger Hackman is?"

"Is that important?"

"It could be. He was one of the last people to see Houston."

The staccato of Giles' tapping pencil increased. "That might explain his call. Roger Hackman is a private investigator."

From the offices of Saxon, Giles, Renfrow and Hoppelwite to the office of Roger Hackman, Confidential Investigations, was a true trip through the looking-glass. Hackman's office was two flights up old wooden stairs in a theater building that now showed X-rated movies.

In the dimly lit hallway, Lyon paused at the head of the stairs. A credit bureau, a dentist and Hackman's office entered off the hall. The stained half-glass door opened with a creak as he entered the office.

Hackman was a short, squat man with deep-set eyes and a gravel voice that now growled into the telephone. "That's the story," he rasped. "The beauty parlor and then the art gallery. You want me to say she went to a motel, O.K., but we can't prove it."

The squat man slammed the receiver down and with myopic eyes looked at Lyon for a moment and, evidently deciding he was a potential client, smiled and motioned him to a chair.

"Mr. Hackman?"

"Yes."

"I understand that you met with Asa Houston the night before he died."

The pudgy man's eyes dimmed as shutters clicked

down. He slowly lit a cigarillo as he studied Lyon. "I might have."

"I know you did." Lyon smiled.

"Houston hired me a couple of times to do confidential work."

"You prepared a report for him recently."

"I might have. Those things are confidential. You must know that."

"I assume you are available for an assignment."

"I might be; depends on the job. My rate is $100 a day plus expenses."

"If you already had a recent report on someone, you'd be a bit ahead of the game, now wouldn't you?"

"I might."

Lyon placed a hundred-dollar bill on the desk. The wages of crime detection come high, he thought; but after all, in a sense it was Houston's money. "I just wonder, Mr. Hackman, if you don't have a report already prepared on Mr. Jim Graves."

The money quickly disappeared as Hackman appeared to be thinking for a minute. "Nope. And like I said, my rate is $100 a day plus expenses. How much of a report do you want?"

Lyon placed another hundred on the desk and inwardly cringed, his natural Yankee frugality objecting with a cry. "I'm really in quite a rush; do you just happen to have a report on Mrs. Houston?"

Again the money disappeared. "It just so happens that I do. Now, since you have hired me to represent you, I can certainly give you a report, right?"

"Of course."

The report appeared on the desk as quickly as the money had disappeared. As he glanced at it, Lyon had an urge to reach for his pen and insert a failing grade. The two pages of single spaced typing were filled with misspelled words, strike-overs and unbelievable syntax. "I'm glad neatness doesn't count," he mumbled.

"You're getting a real bargain. That's a two week surveillance, and you only paid for one day. I ought to charge you one big one."

"I appreciate your special rates, Mr. Hackman," he said and glanced through the report again. "You guarantee the accuracy of this?"

"Sure. I even got pictures, but that'll cost you extra."

At "Sarge's Place" Rocco was so excited that he didn't notice two cars running the stop sign and a band of motorcyclists without crash helmets. With glee he finished the surveillance report and slammed the table.

"We've got the bitch," he said.

Lyon shook his head. "I can't believe it, although it's probably true. I've met the woman, Rocco. She's a cross between Garbo and Bergman . . . womanhood personified, cool, well-bred, vibrant . . . why this . . ." he waved the report, "muck."

"The way the Goddamn thing reads, she'd worked her way through the whole crew of the submarine base and was starting on the Coast Guard Academy. Listen, old buddy, I don't care what she seemed. I could tell you stories 'bout junior league members in little Murphysville that would send you to a monastery."

"I feel very naive."

"It all fits," Rocco said. "Houston gets the investigator's report and hits his wife with it that night. The next morning he makes appointments with his lawyers, accountant and banker. Obviously he planned to dump her."

"We could probably prove that."

"Wifey-poo sees the bread ticket going out the window and knocks him off. Christ, it's practically a textbook case."

Lyon tried to imagine the cool woman he remembered in the drawing room inhabiting a hotel room on many afternoons, while young men at the downstairs bar flipped coins to see who got firsties, seconds and sloppy thirds. A picture of that laughing woman at the head of the long dining table discussing Brecht and Piscator merged with the naked body on soiled sheets, laughing in lust.

"Do we have enough to go to Pat with?" Lyon asked.

"We're getting close," the Chief replied.

"What next?"

"Time for your visit to Miss Helen."

"Because if you go you might get your ass in a sling," Lyon said.

"You read my mind."

"There's just one thing, Rocco."

"What's that?"

"Every time you send me off to see someone they end up dead."

* * *

The cemetery behind the Church of the Redeemer is of sufficient antiquity to attract tombstone rubbers from the farthest corners of New England. Lyon parked at the rear access road, away from the main segment of the funeral procession. He stepped over the low, wrought iron fence and curved his way through the older portion of the cemetery. The faces on many of the upright slabs had been worn smooth by years of rain and wind, while others, judiciously cut deeper into the granite, still held their inscriptions. He never failed to notice the myriad smaller stones clustered around the graves of long dead women—the graves of children, dead in childbirth or ravaged by disease in early childhood.

Lyon hurried away from the older portion of the cemetery toward the new section where neat stones, subdivision like, were aligned in mute uniformity. From a distance he could see the funeral entourage, a tableau of several dozen mourners standing with bowed heads. The Governor, a U.S. Senator, and a member of the cabinet stood with others in appropriate condolent manner at the burial of Asa Houston.

Canon James McFarland, known amongst the Episcopal diocese as being short on theology but long on fund-raising, and known unaffectionately by young curates as "The Cathedral Builder," read from the Book of Common Prayer.

Helen Houston stood next to the Canon. Black became her. As the final words of the service drifted through the trees the mourners eddied away from the grave in small groups, many of them going up to Helen Houston to say a few words of condolence.

Lyon stood next to the lead limousine as Helen Houston moved slowly through the crowd toward him. As she approached the automobile Lyon opened the car door. Expressionless, she glanced up at him and then stepped into the car.

He sat next to her on the wide seat and closed the door. The car started, the uniformed chauffeur slowly weaving the car through the departing mourners. Helen Houston rolled the dividing window up and turned toward Lyon, her eyes appraising him disdainfully.

"I told you on the phone. I have no desire to speak with you," she said.

"You know your husband didn't kill himself," Lyon replied. "You, perhaps more than anyone else, know that it wasn't in keeping with his personality. He was a man of action and decision, not one of retreat."

She turned away from Lyon to look out the window. "It doesn't matter," she said. "He's dead."

Her hips shifted slightly on the seat and Lyon was drawn to the curve of her body, the rounded knees pressed tightly together, the line of her legs and hips and her forward breasts, taut and thrusting.

"He was going to divorce you," Lyon said.

"You have been busy, Mr. Wentworth. Did Mr. Hackman offer to sell you the pictures after I turned him down? He'll probably peddle them to adolescents in some schoolyard."

"I only bought the surveillance report."

"The photographs are much more interesting . . . shall we say, graphic?" she said, turning to him. "A great deal more interesting than times and places."

"And numbers."

"Does it shock you that the lady likes to copulate, that the lady fucks on Friday and stores up screws like coins in a piggy bank?"

"Yes, to be honest. It did shock me."

"You're a prude, Mr. Wentworth, and you look at me like some ancient schoolmaster."

"You were crying when you left his office that day."

She pulled up the sleeve of her dress to reveal long welts along her upper arm. "He could be very nasty," she said without self-pity. "You should see my breasts, Mr. Wentworth; they're a mass of bruises—would you like to see my breasts?"

Lyon realized with a shock that he would, but thrust the thought out of his mind. "Where did you go when you left the office?"

Her hand rested on his thigh and Lyon moved slightly. "Women do different things when they're upset. Some shop, some drink, I fuck." She tapped the glass divider behind the chauffeur. "Henry is very accommodating for those quickies. And, I must admit that in retrospect I received a perverse pleasure in knowing I was getting laid while my husband died."

Her hand moved farther across Lyon's leg, and he shifted in his seat until his back was against the door and further retreat was impossible. "His death came at a very convenient time for you," Lyon said.

"Very convenient," she said as her hands made little flicking motions along his inner leg.

As it slowed for a traffic light, Lyon jumped from the limousine and strained his ankle. Her heard her cool laugh as the car gathered speed and turned the corner.

* * *

"If you don't leave I'm calling the police," Miss Florence Reed said, with her aquiline nose touching the door's safety chain.

"We are the police," Rocco replied.

At a loss for a reply, she hesitated and then took the chain off the door. Rocco and Lyon entered the small apartment, to be overwhelmed by chintz and cats. Chintz curtains, upholstery and wall paper, with an Angora, Persian, Manx and alley cat covering most of the furniture.

She sat primly on the edge of a small divan, her legs pressed tightly together. The pose was slightly reminiscent of Helen Houston's posture in the limousine, and Lyon reflected with guilt on his temptation to stay in the car with the very attractive nymphomaniac. In bed, the previous night, Beatrice had turned her back with a small snort, still angry over Rocco's intrusion and the shattering of their day. Lyon knew this was not Bea's usual form of domestic punishment, and that after tonight he might once again be removed from possible temptation.

"What do you want from me?" she asked.

"Just a few questions, and your help with something," Rocco said.

"Does he have to be here?" she asked, pointing at Lyon.

"I'll try to keep him from attacking you," Rocco said. "Miss Reed, on the morning of Mr. Houston's death, you heard a shot. Can you tell me what happened then?"

"I . . . I ran to the door of his office."

"It's important to us that you remember exactly what happened next."

She thought a moment. "Well, nothing for a while. I began to pound on the door. I could hear the men in the board room pounding on the other door, then the splintering of wood when they broke it in. In a minute or two someone opened my door and let me in . . . it was horrible."

"I see," Rocco said and went on in a quiet manner. "Now, you mentioned to us before that Mr. Houston was very fond of his recording devices, that he insisted that all his executives have devices like his."

"That's true."

"And he had directors' and committee meetings recorded."

"Yes, he did."

"Where would those tapes be kept?"

"In the file room next to my office."

"Would a great many people have access to them?"

"Yes, anyone authorized to be in the executive wing. Someone couldn't just walk in off the street and get them."

"Miss Reed, we'd like to borrow a few of those tapes overnight."

"I couldn't do that without a court order."

"Miss Reed," Rocco said, "what I've asked from you would be a great aid to us. I am sure Mr. Houston, if he were alive, would want you to cooperate."

She looked at him for a long moment. "Do you know, I believe he would."

With a dubious glance, but reassured by a telephone call from Sergeant Pasquale, the security guard escorted Lyon toward the wire shop in Building Seven. That morning the first selectman of Murphysville had ordered Rocco to run a traffic count on Route 66. This had enraged Rocco, not so much because he feared missing the meeting with Lyon this morning, nor did he dislike making neat notations of the types and numbers of passing vehicles. It was the counter's inability to chase traffic violators that bugged him. He had finally helped his depression by establishing a speed trap farther up the highway.

As they entered the wire shop the guard motioned toward a large heat oven where Jim Graves was helping a denim-clad workman feed a metal bar into the carrier tray.

The guard retreated a discreet distance as Lyon watched Graves. The fire door to the oven opened, and the interior white heat illuminated the man's face. As the oven door closed, Graves stepped back and made a minor adjustment to the controls. His concentration was so intense that he failed to notice Lyon a few feet to his side until Lyon tentatively grasped his elbow.

As Graves turned, it took a moment for his concentration to dissipate and for his recognition of Lyon to register. "Wentworth," he finally said. "Glad you found me. How do you like the wire shop?"

"I'm not exactly sure what they're doing."

"The Graves tour, then. I'm proud of this operation." He grasped Lyon's elbow and led him across the plant floor. "The wire shop is my own creation and a new operation for the company. Diversity is the answer, Wentworth. And I don't mean buying other companies like the big conglomerates do. We do it ourselves; each year we add a new product. Wire's only six months old and already we've turned the corner and are in the black."

With pride Jim Graves led Lyon through the shop, and Lyon observed the man's childlike glee as he explained the various operations. He demonstrated how six-foot-long metal bars with high gold content were heated in the oven they'd just passed, and showed Lyon where the bar was drawn through water, heat and die-cutting traps until finally a single strand of wire was run through the last series of cutting dies onto a spool, making a thin, nearly invisible wire of high tensile strength.

"What's it used for?" Lyon asked.

"Rocket circuitry, airplane circuitry, anything electrical that requires strength with a high conductive quality."

They sat in a foreman's office where Graves wiped his perspiring forehead with a handkerchief. "It's very interesting," Lyon said.

"If you like this, you should see the automated line we just opened in Building Three. That's my pride and joy—put everything I know into it and ten years on the plans . . . the most fully automated line in the world."

"I'd like to see it sometime," Lyon said.

"Well, Wentworth, I guess you can tell one thing. I'm a shirt-sleeve executive. Try and spend at least an hour a day on the plant floor, different department every day. Surprising what you can learn. Now, what can I do for you?"

"I just have a couple of questions about the morning Asa Houston was killed."

" 'Killed'? You mean when he killed himself."

Lyon examined the bifocal microscope on the foreman's desk for a moment. "Possibly. You were in the board room next door."

"Yes, I always chair the foremen's meeting."

"Tell me exactly what happened."

"It's all in the police report. We were having our meeting like we do every other Thursday at ten-fifteen sharp when we all heard the shot from Asa's office. We ran to the door, and when he didn't answer we broke it in. That's all."

"Who broke the door in?"

"I'm not sure, Smitty, Wilson . . . several of them. It was pretty much of a madhouse."

"Do you know anything about the Houstons' marriage?"

"Only what's pretty much common knowledge around here."

"You mean about her affairs."

"Oh, I wouldn't know about that. I mean about her working."

"Working?"

"Sure. If I had her in here she could run this shop better than any two engineers I've got. She's also one hell of a fine metallurgist."

"Yes, you told me."

"She liked not working at first. Had a pretty tough time as a kid, I expect, and liked the money. Later on she'd come to me and cry on my shoulder. At first she said it was fine being Asa Houston's newest possession, but she missed working, and he wouldn't let her come back. She tried other places, but the competition wouldn't hire her for obvious reasons, and if she got a job somewhere else Houston would put the word out and she'd be laid off . . . eventually she gave up . . . found other interests, I guess."

"Yes," Lyon said. "I think she found other interests."

"You know, Wentworth, I'm not sure I like your innuendoes about Helen."

"She did have a motive, didn't she?"

"A lot of people did, including me."

"You?"

"Sure. Houston was trying to break my contract and dump me. After thirty years of building production and ten years of work on the automated plant, he tries to dump me."

"Why?"

"Houston Company is a big corporation, public, on the Big Board. We have a bunch of directors who were getting tired of his absentee management. Houston had his hands in a hundred different things, expected me to run the show here for him. There was a movement to kick him upstairs, up to chairman of the board. He thought I was behind it."

"Were you?"

"Yes, Mr. Wentworth, I was. In fact, at tomorrow's board meeting I will be elected president of the company."

Eleven

After the fifth hour of listening to the tapes Florence Reed had obtained for them, Lyon felt he was learning more about the Houston Company than he really cared to know. A great many of the discussions repeated on the recordings were incomprehensible, and others he found either appalling or surprising. The practicality of convertible debentures and lines of credit pegged to two points above prime were an enigma to him, while interminable discussions of unit production and automation were at least comprehensible, even if many of the terms used were foreign. Most surprising were the often heated discussions among the vice-presidents. He had always assumed that corporate decisions were made in a dictatorial fashion with little room for dissenting opinions, and yet he found that sales was constantly at loggerheads with production and that the comptroller seemed to want to keep every penny of the company's money squirreled away in some safe haven.

His mind had wandered and he stopped the tape, reversed it to a section he wanted and stopped the machine. Shuttling forward and backward, he isolated the word he wanted and began to extract it from the tape.

"MY GOD, WHAT IS ALL THIS STUFF?" Bea stood in the doorway of the study, surveying the mass of recording equipment, electronic gear and scattered spools of tape.

Startled, Lyon snipped his finger with the X-acto knife and clenched his teeth. "I am working," he said from the corner of his mouth.

"Oh my, is Santa Claus broadcasting from the North Pole this year?"

Lyon answered without turning to face his wife. "It all has to do with a new book, the Eel and the Electron."

"What happened to Cat?"

"You know how it is, hon. When an idea comes to you, you've just got to push forward with it. This eel is a vibrant character, but it's really an allegory concerning St. Thomas Aquinas."

Bea pushed two boxes of tapes from the seat of the leather chair and plunked into it. "My dear husband, this afternoon I voted on a budget that is several millions above revenues; somehow they convinced me it was the economical thing to do. Now, maybe I can buy an unbalanced budget, but allegories about St. Thomas and eels I don't buy."

"How about the Raccoon and the Recorder?"

"I think you're full of it. You didn't buy all this stuff, did you?"

"A good deal of it is second-hand."

"HOW MUCH?"

"I haven't added it up."

"MAKE A GUESS, AN ESTIMATE, TRY ME."

"Would you believe twenty or thirty dollars?" He knew from the forbidding silence that she didn't believe twenty or thirty dollars. He swiveled the chair to face his wife. She had leaned back to look at him with a bemused smile.

"Try again," she said.

"Twelve hundred and eighty dollars," Lyon said and poured two glasses of sherry.

Bea pulled her always-present notebook from her jacket pocket and began to jot figures. "Twelve hundred and eighty, five hundred for the Florida jaunt, the case of liquor you bought Rocco for a get-well present, two suits of clothing ruined, your doctor bills, gasoline, the publisher's advance that you missed. SIX THOUSAND. SIX THOUSAND, LYON."

"You forgot the five thousand Houston sent."

"Of which you gave half to Rocco. Oh, and I forgot the money you gave that private investigator."

"It's for a good cause."

"I'd call it a rather expensive hobby. So, please tell me what you're doing."

"I think I'm getting ready to kill a Wobbly."

Pat Pasquale arrived before Rocco and sat sullenly in a corner of the living room nursing a scotch and water. Kim snorted and disappeared to her apartment when the unmarked police car pulled into the driveway, and now Bea sat on the sofa looking thoroughly dejected.

"I'm on my own time, Wentworth. So, where's your big friend?" Pat said.

"He had to go over to the State Police barracks and borrow something."

"He borrows and you buy," Bea said. "I wonder if I can get a state civil service job typing envelopes? It would pay better than State Senator, and at this rate we're going to need the money." She turned to Pat. "How's the incidence of forcible rape in Hartford this year, Sergeant?"

"Not bad, Senator. We expect a year-end decrease due to more men on foot. Which is where I'll probably be next week."

Beaming, Rocco Herbert strode into the room. "I've got my end," he announced.

"I refuse to comment on that remark," Pat said.

"My wife will never believe what I'm doing," Pat said.

"I'll set things up," Lyon said.

Pat was on his feet. "Wait just a minute, you two. Let's see if I understand this parlor game we're playing. You guys have two suspects. During the time of the suicide which you call a murder, one was out in the parking lot copulating with the chauffeur and the other was in a meeting in front of fifteen reliable witnesses."

"Exactly," Lyon replied. "And we're going to show you what happened that morning."

The police sergeant looked at them with a skepticism that gradually turned to interest. "You really think you've got something?"

"We do," Rocco said.

"Then I'm interested," the sergeant said.

"All right, then," Lyon said. "Let's imagine that my study is Houston's office, that the windows can't be opened, and that this room is either the secretaries' office or the board room."

"I'm with you so far," Pat said.

"Good. Now, Rocco, if I can borrow your gun." Along with his service revolver Rocco handed Lyon a paper bag. "It's now 8 P.M., but we can imagine it as 10 A.M. It's the time lapse that's important."

"Be careful with that gun," Bea said.

Lyon left the living room, closing the heavy study door securely. He took a stuffed Wobbly doll from the mantel and placed it in his desk chair and inserted a cassette in the recording machine. Glancing at his watch, he turned the recorder on. He took the silencer from the paper bag Rocco had given him and screwed it onto the barrel of the thirty-eight caliber service pistol.

Glancing at the sweep second hand of his watch he pointed the gun at the stuffed toy's head. "Sorry, old chap," he said, "but you're repairable." He fired and the gun went off with a short pop. With stuffing flying through the air, the doll spun upward and landed against the far wall.

He unscrewed the silencer and slipped it in his pocket and laid the pistol on the desk. He threw the switch of the electrical system he'd attached to the edge of the desk that afternoon, and immediately heard the click of tumblers falling into place at the door. The small, airline flight bag was on the mantel in place of the destroyed doll. He picked it up, its deceiving weight almost forcing him to drop it. At the door he passed the bag back and forth across the lock face as the tumblers clicked open.

Leaving the room with the flight bag held behind his back, he held it against the door frame until he was satisfied that the door was again locked. Lyon walked across the living room and poured a sherry.

"Now what?" Pat said.

"We wait," Lyon replied. "I've got it set for five minutes, but it could be any length of time up to ninety minutes. The murderer has just left Houston's office, and Houston, supposedly alone, has locked the doors."

"I'm with you so far," the detective said.

Lyon looked at his watch. "Just about . . ." The loud shot startled the group in the living room. Pat leaped across the room to the study door and fumbled with the handle.

"It's locked," the diminutive detective said.

Rocco picked up the flight bag and walked to the study door. He passed the bag back and forth across the door and then opened it. "We've got ourselves a portable electro-magnet," Rocco said.

"Well, I'll be damned," Pat said as they entered the study.

Bea stood in the doorway and surveyed the mass of stuffing throughout the room. "My God, Lyon, you've made a mess," she said.

Lyon picked up the Wobbly doll and handed it to the detective. From his pocket he took the silencer. "This is on loan with the compliments of the State Police Museum."

"I've got to return it or Norbert will have my head," Rocco said.

"Now the tape," Lyon said and reversed the direction of the cassette player. When the tape passed his pre-determined mark he stopped it and ran it forward on play. "Listen to this."

The voice from the speaker was unmistakably Asa Houston's. "I have come to the end," the tape intoned. "There are few alternatives left, and I am taking the only course of action open to me. Everything is in order, and the lawyers will know where to look." The voice stopped. Weak, hardly discernible noise, then the opening of the drawer. Again silence until the faint click of the revolver's engagement and the shot.

As it had when he'd heard the original tape in the Hartford police station, the shot startled Lyon. The tape continued running—a muffled pounding on a door, and then silence as the cassette reached the end of the spool.

"That's just fine," Pat said. "But how the hell did you steal the tape from my office?"

"We didn't; it's our own."

"It's identical to the one I took from Houston's office that morning," Pat said.

"I know," Lyon said as he inserted another cassette tape in the machine. He ran the machine forward to the spot he wanted and turned up the volume.

"I have come to the end," the voice of Houston intoned. "This crap with the unions is breaking my chops. I'm Goddamn ready to meet with the business reps today if it'll do any good at all."

Lyon switched off the machine. "These tapes," he said and indicated the boxes strewn throughout the room, "come from the Houston Company. It's a chore, but not difficult, to go through and pick out appropriate words and phrases, re-record them with a gunshot and a little door pounding."

For the first time in several days Bea looked pleased. "I get it," she said. "The murderer went into the office earlier, shot him, put the cassette on with the pre-recorded sequence and then left."

"Houston was already dead," Rocco said, "when two dozen witnesses heard a shot and rushed into the room."

"It was all on the cassette," Pat said. "So when I arrived, the machine was still on, and the playing was synchronized to give the murderer the length of time he needed."

"Ah, the light breaks through for the Hartford police," Rocco said.

"The murderer made a mistake," Lyon continued. He inserted the cassette back in the recorder. "Listen to the end once again." He ran the tape to Houston's voice and let it play.

". . . the lawyers will know where to look." The voice stopped. Faint rustling could be heard, then the opening of a drawer, the click of the revolver and the shot.

"So, I . . ." Pat started to say until Lyon put his fingers over his lips. The tape continued in silence until the muffled sound of someone beating on the door and then the tape ran out.

"There's no body falling," Lyon said. "Our friend had a hell of a lot of work to do that night, listening to tapes and re-recording sounds. He or she worked it out beautifully except for staging one sound . . . the body falling. Notice the fidelity of everything else: the sound of the drawer opening, even the revolver. It would have picked up the sound of the gun and the body falling."

Pat walked slowly around the room. He hefted the revolver, flipped open the cylinder and extracted the spent cartridge, then handed the gun back to Rocco. He walked over to the tape recorder, examined it, brushed some stuffing from the desk top and sat at the desk to contemplate the mutilated Wobbly. "You know," he said, "you two guys have done one hell of a job."

"Pure intellect," Rocco said and laughed.

"Only a couple of problems left," Pat said.

"Which one did it?" Bea said. "Helen Houston or Jim Graves?"

"Couple of problems before we get that far," Pat said glumly.

"What's that?" Rocco asked.

"Item one," the small detective said. "The recorder in Houston's office was on when I arrived."

"It was on from the time the murderer turned it on," Lyon said.

"The microphone had the record button depressed. In other words, it would have erased over anything else on the tape. How do you explain that?"

They were silent as Pat walked over to the door and waved the flight bag back and forth over the lock; he admired the clicks as the tumblers fell and opened. "Your electro-magnet idea is fine and dandy," Pat continued. "I can really appreciate it, except that I examined the doors to the room that day. Houston was a bug, a real fanatic about security and industrial espionage. The buildings have back-up security systems everywhere, all sorts of things, including shielded locks."

"Shields?" Lyon asked.

"That's right. He wasn't any amateur, you know. The man was a damn fine engineer and machinist. The door was shielded under the wood veneer. No way your little gadget here would work." He tossed the flight bag back to Lyon. "Any more ideas, guys?"

"Well, back to the drawing board," Lyon said.

* * *

Sunday afternoon Beatrice and Kimberly held the mooring lines securely as Lyon made his pre-flight tests on the balloon. The bag above his head was now filled to tautness and the propane burner was chugging away, pumping more hot air into the balloon envelope. The balloon hovered over the yard at fifty feet, its body straining upward.

Lyon glanced into the sky toward the top of the envelope. It was taut, the sleeve above the burner fluttering at the right inclination and the ripping panel lines secure. He turned and waved at the waiting women and they released the mooring lines.

At first the balloon seemed to bounce upward until, after the initial thrust on release, the rate of ascent normalized to a slow, stately ascent. He flipped the toggle switch on the small citizens' band radio. "Bea, who's following today?"

"Kim will follow in the pick-up truck."

"Fine. The wind's southeast at about four knots. I don't expect a great deal of drift, so ask her to go down route 9 and 9A."

Lyon turned the radio off and attached it securely to the edge of the basket. He made a small adjustment to the propane burner slowing the rate of ascent, and checked the rate of southeast drift. It was a perfect day for ballooning, with only faint wisps of cloud layer many hundreds of feet above, the majority of the sky bluish and clear.

At four thousand feet he stopped the rate of ascent until the balloon seemed to hang motionless in the air, the slight drift hardly perceptible. With the propane burner adjusted to pilot, the world became silent.

"Bunch of Goddamn amateurs playing games," Pasquale had muttered as he left the house the night before. "Stick to traffic violations," he'd yelled back at Rocco as he slammed the car door. "In that area you're a whiz."

The car had driven off with a screech of gravel. Bea had shaken her head while Rocco turned to Lyon.

"Where to now, old buddy?"

"I want to talk to that security captain and the foreman who broke in the door," Lyon said.

"All right," Rocco had replied as he climbed into his car. "I'll pick you up at eight tomorrow."

The security control center for the Houston Company reminded Lyon of the fire control center of a large ship he'd once visited. The major difference was that TV monitor screens replaced the sweeping glow of radar scopes, although the dim room with flickering lights and chairs bolted to the floor in front of monitor banks was similar.

As he greeted them and ushered them into the control center, the security captain had been pleased to see Rocco, a professional who would enjoy the display of gadgetry, and he ignored Lyon. He immediately made Rocco sit in the control chair, and pointed with pride to the various monitors within easy reach of the chair's occupant. They dutifully listened as he explained the security systems, foot patrols, and TV monitoring of over seventy percent of the plant's premises. Finally he had asked what they wanted in the way of further information.

"It's about the doors to Houston's office," Rocco said. "As we understand it, the locks are shielded so that no outside interference can open them."

225

"Of course," the captain had replied. "On Mr. Houston's insistence. Otherwise any decent technician could walk through the plant, opening any locked door or area at will."

"And you're absolutely sure that only two keys existed? You have one and Houston had the other?" Rocco asked.

"I swear to it. My key never left me, and Houston's was found on his body."

"Any chance a duplicate could have been made?" Lyon said.

"Impossible. The lock would have to be removed from the door, which is one hell of a job in itself. A duplicate key for the tumbler system would then have to be manufactured and the lock replaced. My patrol men would have reported any activity of that nature."

"Thank you, Captain," Rocco had said.

They had talked to Ren Wilson, foreman of the automated assembly line, the first man to reach Houston's door after the shot was heard.

"I was at the end of the table, the one near the door to his office," Wilson had told them. "When we first heard the shot we all sort of sat there—stunned. Then a bunch of us ran for the door. Since I was closest I got there first."

"Are you sure the door was locked?" Rocco had asked him.

"Listen, Chief, I'd swear to it on my mother's grave. I musta' tried it half a dozen times before somebody yelled to break it in."

As the balloon drifted slowly along the course of the Connecticut River, Lyon was filled with a huge sense of dejection and depression. How many days had it been since he'd been airborne last, had drifted almost along this same route to take pictures of the grave site? Only a few days ago, and yet they seemed no closer to the solution than they had been when the grave had first been unearthed.

Three bodies found in a grave—one a small child. Martin dead. Now Houston dead. There must be a key somewhere. A key? Lyon laughed aloud.

He had it. The whole thing fit. The simplicity of the scheme was its very beauty. Now, with this last piece of information in place, the whole murder of Houston fell into an answer. He and Rocco hadn't been far wrong; all the details except the door and the recorder had been correct, and now, with the answer, proof would be available.

Lyon looked over the edge of the balloon basket, impatiently scanning the terrain below for a suitable landing area. The balloon had descended to level flight at just below four thousand feet and had drifted several miles downriver. On both sides of the river the land rose harshly from the water's edge to granite and traprock ridges. He would have to wait until the balloon drifted farther east in order to find a relatively flat piece of ground to use for descent.

The increase of the engines to full throttle first brought the airplane to Lyon's attention. Shading his eyes, he glanced toward the sound, but the glare of the sun made the plane invisible in the penumbra.

A hundred feet from the leading edge of the balloon the plane banked sharply into a deep turn. After completing the steep turn, the two-engine Cessna adjusted course for a direct heading at the balloon. Its position and altitude would carry it directly overhead on a pass across the envelope.

He'd had private planes play cat and mouse before, but none as dangerously close as this one. He wondered if the pilot knew that if the plane's propellers should hit the balloon envelope or rigging, the balloon would immediately deflate and the rigging would hopelessly foul the plane's propellers, to plummet both vehicles to earth.

Engine pitch abruptly changed as the pilot throttled back to slow his pass over the balloon. Lyon could only estimate the distance from envelope to plane fuselage as slightly less than fifty feet. Past the balloon the plane eased into a slow 360-degree bank that once again placed it on a direct tangent toward the balloon.

The pilot had made a slight adjustment in altitude so that the new pass would carry the plane directly over the balloon with less clearance than before. Fear stabbed at Lyon. This was not some pseudo hot-shot pilot playing air games with a new and unfamiliar quarry. The repeated passes, each one at lower altitude, made it quite clear that the plane's pilot had the destruction of the balloon as a primary objective.

He flipped the toggle switch of the raid. "Kimberly. Kim. Come in, are you there?"

"Hello, Big Chief, this is Red Marble."

"Listen, kids, get off the band," Lyon said with as much control as he could muster. "This is an emergency."

"I always call Big Chief at three," was the plaintive reply.

"Please get off the band for a minute," Lyon said as the plane made another pass over the top of the balloon.

"Is masta' ready to descend from the heavens?" Kim said.

"Knock it off, Kim. There's some joker up here playing Red Baron with me. Get to a telephone and call Rocco. It can only be our friend."

She sensed the panic in his voice and dropped her sarcasm. "Do you have the plane's I.D. number?"

"Just a minute." He took field glasses from the side of the basket and searched the skies. The plane was coming out of the sun again at a speed that would be close to a stall. As the plane side slipped slightly to correct approach position, he picked out the numbers on the wing and radioed them to Kimberly on the ground.

"I've got them," she replied. "I can see you about two miles away from my position. From here it looks like the plane will hit you."

He crouched down in the rocking basket as the plane, almost directly overhead, approached the top of the balloon. Around the trailing edge of the plane's wings, liquid poured in a slim, steady stream as the plane passed a few feet over the top of the balloon.

As rivulets of liquid coursed down the side of the balloon envelope, a drop fell on Lyon's hand. He tasted it—gasoline. The airplane's fuel caps were off, and gasoline was siphoning out of the wing tanks, successfully covering a good portion of the balloon's skin with gasoline.

The plane banked and approached the balloon again in what Lyon knew would be the final pass. He could see the hand extended from the pilot's window with the flare gun poised.

As the flare hit the top of the balloon the gasoline broke into flames with a clap. The plane's engines whined with throttle increase.

Looking directly upward through the sleeve into the interior of the balloon envelope, Lyon could see through the micro-thin sheen of the top surface that fire burned along the rigging of the upper circumference. Now, along the sides of the balloon, fire approached the basket as it burned steadily along rigging lines.

He grabbed the emergency lines leading to the ripping panel and pulled them quickly downward with all the leverage he could muster. A large portion of the side envelope immediately peeled away and the balloon lurched sideways and downward.

Grasping the sleeve immediately over his head, he yanked it from the envelope, allowing more hot air to escape. Glancing at the altimeter, he saw his height at thirty-two hundred feet with a quick rate of descent. The immediate danger would be quick explosion of the whole envelope, in which case he knew that the remaining portion of the balloon, basket, and himself would immediately plummet earthward.

His only chance lay in a rapid rate of descent before explosion and complete destruction of the envelope. As large quantities of hot air escaped through the hole caused by the ripping panel, the bag began to sag.

Two thousand feet and falling quickly. He hurriedly tried to calculate the rate of descent, the critical survival factor.

Several of the rigging ropes on the right side of the envelope broke away above the supporting ring, and one end of the basket dipped precariously.

Thirteen hundred feet. The slanted downward trajectory of the balloon slid along the path of the Connecticut River. He looked skyward and could see the airplane disappearing rapidly over the northern rim of hills.

Eight hundred feet. The rate of descent was faster than any he had ever experienced. From above he could hear portions of the envelope shredding. As more rigging lines gave way, the basket tilted further to an almost vertical position. With both hands he grabbed the supporting ring overhead and held on, knowing that it would remain until the last line parted.

He was below the hill and ridge line to each side of the river. The altimeter and other instruments had fallen from the basket, but he esitmated height at two or three hundred feet above the north-south line of the river.

If it held for a few more seconds he would reach the water. Then the danger would be in becoming enmeshed in the envelope and remaining rigging lines, many of which now flapped dangerously.

Thirty feet above the waterline Lyon let go of the supporting ring and dropped free from the balloon.

He hit the water feet first, and the impact shuddered through his body. His feet brushed river bottom silt, and looking upward he could see the translucent surface light far above, as he began the slow and interminable rise to the waterline.

He gasped for air as his head broke the surface and

he weakly trod water. Turning toward downstream, the path of the balloon, he saw that the surface was undisturbed. The balloon had either exploded before striking the water, or else had sunk immediately.

The shoreline was over a hundred yards away and it might have been ten miles, he thought, as he began slow strokes through the water. A fisherman in a small boat rowed nonchalantly toward him and Lyon raised an arm, shocked to see for the first time that his arms were blackened and burned.

The fisherman's oars dipped cleanly through the water as he approached. "I've heard of balls of fire," the man said as he pulled alongside Lyon, "but that was ridiculous."

Twelve

The ghosts of Lyon Wentworth held him tightly by the hands. The two little girls, one with hair of gold, the other dark as night, led him across the grassy field.

"Come on, Daddy," the gold one cried and pulled him forward.

"Show us the Wobblies," the dark-haired child said.

They pulled him through the field of new-mown grass. In the distance he saw their house, Bea standing on the porch beckoning to them as the wind whipped her dress.

"I have to go, children," he said. They squeezed his hands tightly and he winced in pain.

"Don't go," they cried in unison. "Don't go."

But he left them and walked through the yellow, swirling fog.

Bea stood next to the hospital bed crying. "I don't know whether to kiss you," she said through tears, "or chew you out for destroying your eight-thousand-dollar toy balloon."

Lyon fought his way through a haze of morphine. The small hospital room was filled with blurred edges; a yellow halo surrounded Bea where she stood at the head of the bed. In slow motion the room returned to focus. He tried to sit up, but fell back on the pillow as a wrenching pain racked his neck and shoulders.

"What time is it?" he asked.

"Seven."

"Night or day?"

"Night. You know, Lyon, if you're going to spend half your life in the water, you'll need advanced swimming lessons."

He smiled, and that hurt also. ". . . it does seem to be becoming a habit. Did they get the pilot of the plane?"

"Kim got through to Rocco, the State Police were notified, and as far as I know, they covered all the local airports from Massachusetts to past New Haven."

"Good. If they made it in time they should have our friend."

"I certainly hope so. You know, dear husband, I'm introducing a bill tomorrow in the Senate. No middle-aged balloonists who write children's books are allowed to chase murderers."

"That narrows it down," he smiled, "except that I'm not middle-aged."

"A strong case could be made for that," she said.

Lyon pulled his white-mittened hands from under the sheets and examined them. The bandages covered many of the fingers and reached upward to his elbows. "I didn't even realize I was burned," he said. "What happened?"

"By the grace of God and a passing fisherman, you were saved. I don't think you could have made it to shore by yourself."

"I'm not sure I could have either. You know, if our friend keeps this up, he's going to make me angry."

"You keep this up and you'll be dead or divorced—or both."

"Come here," Lyon said and Bea sat dutifully on the edge of the bed. He surrounded her with bandaged hands and pulled her toward him. She kissed him on the forehead as he nuzzled her neck.

"There's probably a city ordinance against doing that in a hospital bed," Rocco said from the doorway.

Flushing, Bea jumped off the edge of the bed. "I told you," she said, "he's haunting us like some overgrown specter."

"Don't you like me, Beatrice?"

"I love you, darling, but you turn up at the damndest times."

"You two can exchange pleasantries later," Lyon said. "Did they get my friend, Rocco?"

"No," the large man replied. "We covered all the airports as quickly as we could, but the plane landed in nearby Plainville, minutes after you went into the drink."

"The plane? Whose is it?"

"The ident shows that it belongs to the Houston Company. We found it parked at the far end of the runway, but that's a small airport and no one is sure who took it up or brought it down."

"Who had access to the plane and is a licensed pilot?"

"Helen Houston and Jim Graves are both pilots and both have used the plane on numerous occasions," Rocco said.

"Pick them both up," Bea said. "Somebody tried to kill Lyon."

"We've tried," Rocco said. "Neither Helen nor Graves

can be found. We've got their homes staked out and a APB out for both of them."

"Could they be in this together?" Bea asked.

"I don't think Graves would have enough spunk in the bunk for Helen Houston. No, I don't think so," Rocco said.

Painfully, Lyon sat up and swung his feet toward the floor. Swiveling his head several times, he discovered that the neck and back pain was bearable. Standing, he felt foolish in the short hospital gown, and the bandaged hands made him feel awkward.

"Where do you think you're going!" Bea yelled.

"I'm a member of your constituency and need your help," Lyon said. "Now, help me get my pants on."

The Murphysville police cruiser edged toward eighty miles per hour as it sped toward the shore. Rocco Herbert drove with casual ease, one arm resting on the window frame, the other hand lightly caressing the steering wheel.

At one point a State Police cruiser had pulled into the lane behind them and had given chase until Rocco switched on the blinking red roof lights. The state car turned off with a parting toot of its horn.

"You know, Rocco," Lyon said, "there's a distinct advantage in driving from point to point with you—unadulterated, suicidal speed."

"You said you were in a hurry," the large man replied and inched the speedometer toward ninety. "You really think your friend will be in New London?"

"It's worth a try."

The Sequnquit Hotel had known its good days, seventy years before. Now its white facade was sun-peeled along the upper edges, and the small lobby had given up pretensions thirty years ago. The over-stuffed chairs, lumpy from protesting springs, were covered in a film of dust. To the right, off the lobby, a bar created the only vitality in the ancient building. A juke box blared country music and western as young Iowa-born sailors drank pitchers of beer.

"I'll check in here," Rocco said and slipped into the bar.

Lyon had to tap lightly on the counter to catch the attention of the clerk engrossed in an ancient copy of *Playboy* magazine. The clerk looked at him without interest until Lyon slipped a crumpled ten-dollar bill across the scarred counter. He inwardly winced and vowed not to inform Beatrice of his latest expenditure. He did realize, with a start, that he was getting better at this sort of thing.

"Where's Our Lady of Fatima?" Lyon asked.

"Room 412," the clerk replied and slipped the bill into the magazine.

The small, self-service elevator had last been inspected in 1948 and rose the four flights in short jerky movements. It would be the irony of life, Lyon thought, to have plummeted four thousand feet earlier in the day only to die in a four-story elevator accident. The elevator eventually stopped and he pushed the creaking gate and protesting door open.

He walked slowly down the broad hallway with its worn carpet—reminiscent of a more affluent era. The door to room 412 was unlocked and he stepped into the room.

The nude young man sprang toward Lyon with upraised fists. "Hey, I'm not finished, damn it!" he yelled.

"Leave him alone, honey," Helen Houston said from the bed. "He's a special one I've been expecting."

Lyon leaned against the wall as the young sailor threw on his clothes while muttering obscenities about pimps and bitches. Helen turned languorously on the bed and propped her head with one hand. Her firm breasts were pointed with erect nipples, and she ran one hand along her thigh.

As the sailor slammed out of the room she turned on her back. "I knew I'd get you by and by," she said and spread her legs.

"How long have you been here?" Lyon asked. He wiped the beads of perspiration from his forehead with a bandaged hand.

"Oh, ages and ages, baby..I have to have fun and games for a while before I really get started." She stood and walked across the room toward him with a pronounced sway to her hips. "Does it bother you?" She ran her hands along Lyon's body. "I'll take a shower and get all squeaky clean ... and then ..."

"When did you get here?"

"This morning," she said as her hands slipped under his shirt.

"That's true," Rocco said from the doorway. He shook his head as he crossed the room to the bed and threw a blanket at Helen. "She's taken on half the Atlantic Fleet since this morning."

❈ ❈ ❈

238

The police cruiser was going due west with Rocco's usual high rate of speed when he turned to Lyon with a smile. "She had a great body," he said. "Of course I'm trained not to notice such things, but just where would you be if I hadn't been along?"

"In trouble," Lyon said.

"You knew it wasn't her all the time—why the damn trip down here? Or were you bent on seeing her in the buff?"

"No, just a loose end. Now we know; it's Graves without a doubt. It all fits, Rocco, every damn piece."

"He's heard the news by now; he knows you're alive, and that we're after him. He's probably halfway to Brazil."

"I don't think so," Lyon said. "I think I know exactly where to find Jim Graves."

There was a disquieting atmosphere about the closed industrial plant. Spotlights mounted on the corners of buildings illuminated large swatches of space, leaving slivers and corners in darkness. The chain link fence surrounding the property shone silver in the reflection of lights, while the front administration building was bathed in light from ground-mounted lamps. The hum of high-tension wires overhead implied a dormant power.

The gate guard called the night security captain, and he stood in the administration building doorway as Rocco pulled the cruiser into a parking space. Painfully, the two of them limped from the car and climbed the steps.

They followed the captain through the quiet corridors toward the security center. The room was dark except for the multi-faced glow of television monitors. The screened pictures flickered and changed as the mobile cameras, spotted throughout the plant, made their continuous sweeps.

"Are you sure he isn't in his office, or anywhere else in the administration building?"

"Positive, Chief. After you called, I had one of my men make a complete search of this building."

"But he is here?" Lyon said.

"Nothing unusual about Mr. Graves coming in after second shift goes off. He often just walks through the place, sometimes even runs some quality control. What's going on here anyway?"

"We'll fill you in later," Rocco said. "Let's find him first." The large man sat at the console. "I understand you can see most of the plant from here with these gizmos."

"Most, except for the ladies' lounge," the captain said and laughed.

"Knock out the humor and show me how to work the damn things."

The security captain bent over Rocco and showed him how each monitor had a dial for movement and focus. He explained that although the cameras were pre-set, they could be individually hand-operated to expand the viewing area.

They found Jim Graves after manipulating the fourth camera. "Can you focus for a close shot?" Lyon asked.

"Sure." The captain turned a dial. Jim Graves was clearly in focus on the monitor. He was bent over a drafting table near a work console, hurriedly rolling blueprints and stuffing them into cardboard tubes. The yellow dial lights of the console cast an odd glow across his face.

"That's the automated plant," Lyon said. "Where is it?"

"He's at the control panel of Building Three. Why do you suppose he went there?" the guard asked.

"I knew he wouldn't leave without his prints and plans," Lyon said.

"Keep him in focus," Rocco said and reached for a nearby telephone. "I'm having the gates sealed and calling in the city police."

Lyon slipped out the rear door and hobbled down the corridor as fast as painful muscles allowed. It was a hundred yards to Building Three, and he grotesquely loped the distance, at one point falling to his knees as the muscles of his lower back gave out. Stumbling to his feet, he continued in cold anger.

Building Three was the largest in the entire factory complex. Many of the warehouses and subsidiary buildings fed material and parts into Three by conveyors, runways and loading docks. He remembered that this was the main assembly area, that pre-assembled parts, sub-contractual parts and hundreds of other increments necessary for final engine assembly were destined for final routing to Building Three.

The main entrance of the building was locked, and as Lyon rounded the corner of the building, away from the periphery of light, he stumbled over a crate and cried out in pain as he again broke his fall with injured hands.

The door through the right loading dock was slightly ajar and he slipped into the dim interior. His entry was into a supply area where parts bins stretched to the ceiling. Through the entrance onto the main floor he could see the dim interior of the main assembly area.

Work lights, high on side walls, spaced every twenty or thirty feet, cast small areas of light along the major walkways, while dark machines and unimates loomed in the center darkness.

The perpendicular arms of the strange unimates loomed in unfamiliar shapes. Skeletal outlines of overhead conveyor belts broke the dim work light patterns into odd pentagonal shapes on the hard floor. His breath was coming in choking gasps, and Lyon stopped and leaned against a pillar.

Both in the board room and also in the entrance to the administration building large photographs of Building Three in full operation hung on display. Most of the pictures were taken from a high angle at the end of the building and showed the assembly line stretching several hundred yards. He closed his eyes momentarily to visualize the photographic details, placement of machinery and full interior structure of the building.

As he recalled, engine blocks started on the line to the rear of his present position. As the blocks moved slowly through the plant interior, they stopped for varying times at assembly stations along the way. At these points conveyors fed parts to the assembly area while automated machinery or workers performed the necessary functions.

The text below the pictures of Building Three pointed with pride to the extent of automation in the plant, that fewer workers were required than at any similar engine assembly plant in the world. That, in fact, one skilled man operating the console, with computer connections, could perform many of the plant's functions.

The television image in the security center showed Graves huddled over a bank of dials in a glass-enclosed booth. The control center—where was it? Crossing to the center of the floor at the main assembly area he climbed atop a work bench. The additional four feet of height allowed him to see over much of the looming machinery and material.

In a far distant corner, slightly raised off the assembly floor, he saw the glass operation center with the vague form of a man in its interior.

"That's you, isn't it, Wentworth?"

The voice echoed and reverberated throughout the large building. "I'm glad it's you, Wentworth, you son-of-a-bitch. Very glad it's you."

The public address system must have had speakers every few feet to overcome the noise when the plant was in operation. Lyon climbed off the work bench and started up the aisle toward the distant control center.

In neatly aligned overhead banks, the full interior lights began to come on. As switch after switch was thrown, the building was lit in sections to daytime intensity.

The hum of power surrounded Lyon as the assembly line began to inch slowly forward. The room had come alive with pulsating machinery. Throughout the building, machines gathered speed and momentum—

automatic welders began to beat a staccato, while conveyor belts carried parts uselessly to the line.

Lyon stopped a hundred yards from the control booth. Graves' outline was now quite clear as he stood before the large console, arms akimbo, watching the line with an unnatural patience. The distant man shrugged and sat in a chair before the dials as Lyon walked toward him.

A jungle of machinery moving in ways foreign to him surrounded him on all sides. The prey sat in his perch unperturbed, seemingly unconcerned, and turned to the dials that made the room alive to his touch.

A conveyor overhead whined as its speed increased.

Lyon threw himself quickly to the side and bounced off a vending machine as the steel block, released directly over the spot where he'd been standing, crashed to the floor.

"Missed you, Wentworth." The voice laughed through two dozen speakers throughout the building.

A waist-high cart with six wheels scuttled down the aisle, narrowly missing the crumpled steel of the fallen engine block. It swiveled on two rear wheels and positioned itself a few yards in front of Lyon.

He waited until the last possible moment before throwing himself sideways. The cart crashed into the vending machine and crumpled the light metal of the machine. The automatic cart immediately began to reverse direction for another run at Lyon as the laughter crashed throughout the plant.

Ahead and to the right was a parts bay with a parked fork lift. Lyon ran toward the lift as overhead conveyors, with a series of large blocks suspended underneath, began to move forward, and the cart swiveled on its wheels to find a proper angle of attack.

The keys were in the fork lift. Lyon clambered on to the driver's seat and almost fell sideways as the delivery cart crashed into the side of the lift. The lift started on the first try. He backed it into the aisle and turned the wheel quickly, swiveling it into position.

The conveyor belt released a block directly over his head and the steel crashed onto the protective mesh at the top of the fork lift.

Lyon threw the small vehicle into gear as another car scuttled in his path and headed directly toward him. Raising the prongs of the lift slightly, he continued forward toward the cart.

The beveled front edges of the prongs dug into the small cart and brought it to a halt. Lyon reversed the cart, disengaged the prongs from the now useless automated vehicle, and threw the lift into forward.

The control booth was only yards to his front, the contorted face of Graves viewing him with a combination of alarm and hate.

Lyon swiveled the lift to the side of the aisle as parts and pieces of machinery crashed along his path. He raised the forks of the lift several feet and threw the small machine into its greatest acceleration.

In the instant before the forks penetrated the glass of the control booth, Graves raised his arms protectively and screamed. As the lift ground to a halt against the supporting structure of the booth, Lyon threw the lever, lowering the forks.

The crushed man in the booth's interior screamed and continued screaming as Lyon laid his head over the steering wheel and closed his eyes. The screaming changed in pitch until words were audible.

"Myself," Graves yelled. "I'll run the whole thing myself. I don't need anyone . . . don't need anyone . . ."

Lyon crawled from the fork lift and fell to the floor, where his hands ground painfully into glass shards from the booth's shattered windows. He pulled himself over the edge of the booth toward the incoherent man. The forks of the lift had lowered across Graves' legs and hips, crushing bone and cartilage.

Black waves poured across Lyon's eyes as he crawled toward the stricken man. Graves turned toward him, his eyes wide and glazed with shock.

"The little girl," Lyon said. "The little girl, what about her?" He bent his head close to the moving lips.

Distant voices were yelling, and then large gentle hands were on his back.

"WE OUGHT TO RESERVE THIS ROOM ON A PERMANENT BASIS," Bea yelled and wilted into a nearby chair. Her concern had turned to exhaustion, and Kimberly stood by her side and ran a reassuring hand over Bea's forehead, while Lyon wondered if perhaps the wrong person wasn't in the hospital bed.

"For a man who lives a quiet life, you sure get around," Kim said. "I'd hate to be with you when you come out of seclusion."

"How about the Moose and the Murderer?" Lyon tried to grin, but it hurt too much.

"No, more like the Iguana and the Idiot," Bea said bleakly and managed a half-smile.

Lyon wrinkled his nose and tried to scratch it with

246

his rebandaged hands, but could only manage a few passing sweeps. He wondered guiltily if the hospital would charge him for two days—one for his earlier stay and unauthorized departure, and now for his recent re-entry. Since they had had to bandage him twice, he supposed it would be for the two days.

"Is it over?" Bea asked weakly.

"Almost," Lyon replied. "We'll know soon, although I'd rather he didn't die."

The door slammed against the wall as Rocco limped in laughing and carrying two magnums of champagne.

"What in hell's so funny? How's Graves?" Lyon asked.

"They're still trying to put him back together. Pat's with him and will let us know as soon as they can tell if he'll make it."

"And that's funny?" Bea asked.

"No, no," Rocco said as he popped a cork and began to pour. "I just got word that Helen Houston's been busted for impairing the morals of a dozen sailors."

"THAT'S SEXIST," Bea said indignantly.

"Not in Helen's case. Seems that the train of sailors weren't all drawn by the beauty of an older woman. She was paying them."

"Can they do anything to her?" Kim asked.

"I don't know," Rocco chortled. "They'll probably declare her off limits to the Atlantic Fleet."

Kim held a paper cup of champagne and stared abstractly into the bubbles rising to the top. "I don't understand all this," she said. "Then Houston did kill the Meyerson family?"

"No," Lyon replied.

"Then it was Bull Martin after all?" Kim asked.

"Wrong again," Lyon said.

"Do I get eighteen more guesses or are you going to tell me?"

Bea began to look interested. "ALL RIGHT, YOU GUYS," she said. "You've dropped one shoe and told us part of it, now let's hear the whole thing."

Pat Pasquale came into the room and with bird-dog precision made for the champagne. Rocco poured him a cup which he immediately drank. "He's busted up, but going to make it," he said. "You did one hell of a job on him, Lyon, but Graves has come through shock and the rest will be uphill."

Lyon lay back on the pillow with a sigh. "Thank God for that."

"Christ, Pat, you should have seen it," Rocco said. "The Black Knight here, mounted on his fork lift, was jousting with half the machinery in that Goddamn place." He turned to Lyon. "You know, old buddy, you could have waited. We were practically right behind you."

"The bastard made me mad as hell," Lyon said.

"Well, anyway," Pat continued, "for the last hour Graves has been babbling like a brook. Half of it's incoherent, part of it's a lot of ranting and raving about starting an automated plant in Brazil, and part of it's begging the Great God of machinery to forgive him for screwing up and knocking off a lot of people."

"Do you have enough for an indictment?" Rocco asked.

"We've already charged him with the attempted murder of Wentworth. He's babbled on about Houston and the Meyersons. An indictment?" He shrugged.

Bea rose in an open state of indignation. "What in hell do you mean indictment question mark?" Her face was flushed with anger. "He did it, didn't he?"

"Of course he did," Rocco said.

"That's right," Pat continued. "You know he did it, I know he did it, half the personnel in this hospital knows he did—but he's talking under medication, without benefit of counsel. I doubt that I can use a word he's told us against him."

"That's crazy," Kim snorted.

"I thought you were the queen of the Civil Rights movement, kid?" Rocco said.

"What do you mean?" Kim asked.

"It works both ways," Rocco replied.

"You must have enough for murder one on the Houston killing," Lyon said. "We outlined everything for you."

"Sure," Pat said and poured more champagne. "Almost enough, if you guys can figure how in hell he got out of that damn room."

"Will somebody tell me what's going on here?" Bea said.

Lyon lay back in the bed and closed his eyes momentarily, the terror and fear of the factory beginning to dissipate.

"The key, Wentworth," the little detective said. "Give me a plausible answer on that one and I've got enough for murder one, even without his confession."

"We overly complicated the whole thing," Lyon said. "It couldn't have been simpler."

"Would you mind, Lyon? Since I've spent half my recent life chasing after you and standing over hospital beds, will you please tell me what's going on?" Bea said.

"Let's start with the Meyersons," Lyon said.

"That's just fine," his wife replied.

"Back in 1943 Meyerson and Bull Martin were the only foremen Houston had," Lyon said. "At a crucial point in the life of the business a batch of engines ready for shipment are discovered to be defective. Now, who knows about this and what happens to them? Coop, the government inspector, knows, and of course notifies Houston. Coop told me that Graves was working with him during the testing process. Graves knows, as do the two foremen, Martin and Meyerson. Bull's no problem and is bought off cheaply. Coop succumbs to the good life and that takes care of him. Graves sees a hell of a lot to his advantage in the situation and rides along on the promises of future gains made by Houston. Meyerson's the problem—so much so that Bull Martin physically has it out with him on the factory floor."

"Then Bull did kill the family?" Bea said.

"No. But Bull thought he had, or at least thought he'd killed Meyerson. Bull was smashed out of his mind, drunk as a lord when he went over to the trailer that night. He did beat Meyerson senseless and then collapsed himself. Graves is right behind him and sees a golden opportunity to become senior man in the factory in one swoop; Graves kills Meyerson and his wife with the stove ring and disposes of the bodies. The next morning when Bull wakes up he tells Bull that he did it—and then he, Graves, pretends he's covering for Bull."

250

"Which explains why Bull almost immediately joined the Army," Rocco said.

"Exactly," Lyon continued. "As far as he was concerned, he thought he was a murderer, and it didn't take too much prodding from Graves to get him to leave."

"Helped along by a few dollars pay-off money from Houston," Bea said.

"You've got it, honey," Lyon said. "Houston accepts the story, probably because he wanted to, that Bull's threat drove Meyerson out of town."

"The little girl," Bea said. "What about the little girl?"

"That was an accidental necessity. She was hiding in the trailer under the bed, clutching her Sonja Henie doll, and Graves didn't discover her until he got the trailer out to the lake."

"Then he had to kill her," Rocco said.

"Had to?" Lyon mused. "I suppose he thought he had to—and did, which explains why she still had the doll in her hands in the grave."

"How horrible," Bea said.

"When we come on the case," Rocco said, "Graves tips off Bull that we're closing in on him. Bull, thinking he was the killer, comes after the two of us."

"And I conveniently removed him," Lyon said.

"But why, Lyon? Killing three people to get a promotion to foreman doesn't make much sense," Bea said.

"More than foreman. Look at Graves' situation. Meyerson and Bull are out of the way, he's in bed with Houston as a most loyal employee, and, in addition, the guy has a real thing about the factory. As far as I can calculate quickly, over the years he benefited monetarily to the extent of some three million dollars."

"Three million?" Pat said incredulously.

"Sure. He drew an average salary of $80,000 per year, plus stock options which were very lucrative while they were growing . . . and eventually he did become president of the company. Compare that to what would have happened if Meyerson had blown the whole story of the defective parts."

"That's fine and dandy," Pat said. "Murphysville has neatly solved its thirty-year-old crime, but that still leaves me with a three-day-old murder."

"Wait a minute," Lyon said. "Let me finish."

"Please do," the little detective said sarcastically.

"After we traced the bodies and I returned from Florida with the affidavit, Houston began to put the whole thing together. He was a bastard in many ways, unscrupulous, tough, closed his eyes to a lot; but it was obvious to him that only Graves could have killed the Meyerson family. After all, he knew one thing we didn't."

"What's that?" Bea asked.

"He knew that he hadn't done it. At that point he decided to cover his flank and get Graves the hell out of the company."

"I'm with you so far," Pat said. "He calls Graves in and informs him that he's getting his walking papers."

"Right," Lyon said. "And that night Graves prepares the recording. He knew the foremen's meeting was scheduled the next morning, and he knew that Houston kept a gun in his desk."

"Exactly as we duplicated it," Rocco said. "Graves goes in the room, shoots Houston with the silencer, puts the gun down after pressing prints on it, and turns on the recorder, with the suicide shot timed perfectly."

"Helen Houston's going into the office that morning was icing on the cake for Graves," Lyon said.

"Goddamn it, the key!" Pat said. "We're right back to where we were the other night at your house."

"No," Lyon said quietly. "Graves used Houston's key."

"I found it on the body myself," Pat said.

"Of course you did," Lyon said. "Graves shoots him, turns the recorder on and takes the key. He locks the door with the automatic switch, but then lets himself out through the board room with the key, locking the door behind him."

"Wait a minute, just one minute." Pat was on his feet pacing the floor excitedly. "The men at the meeting hear the shot and break the door in . . . once inside it's a milling mass of people . . . Graves puts the key back in Houston's pocket."

"And turns the recorder microphone to record," Rocco said.

"What could be simpler," Lyon said.

She stood at the foot of the steps at Nutmeg Hill, her eyes wide, small back straight. Lyon went down the few steps toward her as almond eyes followed closely. He took the little Korean girl in his arms and carried her into the house where the Wobblies were.

The ghosts of Lyon Wentworth, one with hair of gold, the other dark, finished their tea party by the weather vane on top of the barn and began to disappear forever.